A BLAZING HAIL OF BULLETS!

Clint reloaded, realizing he was pinned down good. He couldn't even make it back into the saloon. All he had between the rest of the deputies and himself was a horse trough that was punched full of holes.

He sighted down on one of Tolliver's Deputies and fired. With all the shooting going on he couldn't tell if he hit anything or not, but it was too late to worry . . .

THE GUNSMITH

153

TOLLIVER'S DEPUTIES

J. R. ROBERTS

JOVE BOOKS, NEW YORK

TOLLIVER'S DEPUTIES

A Jove Book / published by arrangement with
the author

PRINTING HISTORY
Jove edition / September 1994

ISBN: 0-515-11456-1

A JOVE BOOK®
Jove Books are published by The Berkley Publishing Group,
200 Madison Avenue, New York, New York 10016.
JOVE and the "J" design are trademarks
belonging to Jove Publications, Inc.

PRINTED IN THE UNITED STATES OF AMERICA

10 9 8 7 6 5 4 3 2 1

THE GUNSMITH

153

TOLLIVER'S DEPUTIES

ONE

Clint Adams had been in Ryland, Kansas, four days before he heard about Daniel Tolliver. He'd stopped while passing through to play some poker. Two days later, he was still doing too well at poker to want to leave.

By the third day he was not only doing well at poker, but also doing extremely well with a young woman named Lydia Burdette. Lydia worked at the general store, which was owned by her father and mother. On his second day in town, Clint had gone in to make a purchase, had struck up a conversation and invited the comely young lady for lunch. He hadn't expected to end up in bed with her by the end of the day, and he was right— it was not until the evening of the third day that they tumbled into his bed, and it was at her insistence. It seemed that

1

Miss Burdette was not the innocent, inexperienced young thing that everyone in town seemed to think. Clint found out that she was quite skilled in bed and eager to show off those skills to someone who could appreciate them.

So by the time the fourth day came around, Clint Adams was thinking that Ryland wasn't a bad little town.

Then he heard about Daniel Tolliver.

"Heard Daniel Tolliver's comin' to town," one of the poker players said.

The game was taking place at the Ryland Saloon. Clint was playing four locals who had thought that by letting a stranger into the game they'd be able to fleece him pretty good. They were finding out differently.

"I heard some talk the sheriff might call him in after all," Fenton Burdette said. He was Lydia's father. He was also a member of the town council—as were all of the other local players.

"Has there been some trouble in town that I don't know about?" Clint asked.

"There was," said Emerson Boone. He owned the town's feed and grain. Like the others, he was in his late forties or early fifties. "Seemed to slack off a bit when you got to town, but I heard there was some trouble last night."

"I didn't hear anything," Clint said, but then he'd been pretty busy with Lydia Burdette.

"We got us a bunch of rowdies in town, Adams," Burdette said, "and it seems the sheriff ain't equipped to handle them himself, so he's calling in Dan Tolliver and his deputies."

Now the name rang a bell with Clint.

"Tolliver's Deputies?"

"That's right," Burdette said.

"They're a bunch of gunmen."

"We heard Tolliver was a marshal," a third man, Sam Wyatt, said.

"Self-styled marshal, you mean," Clint said.

"What's that mean?" Wyatt asked.

"He had a marshal's badge made up, pinned it on himself, then had six deputy badges made and gave them to his men. They're nothing but paid gunmen."

"Sounds like you don't approve of them," Emerson Boone said.

"I don't."

"That sounds odd comin' from a man of your reputation, Adams," Burdette said.

Clint gave the man a hard stare.

"My reputation's got nothing to do with it, Burdette. I don't hire out to kill people."

"Way we hear it," Les Kane, the local banker, said, "they uphold the law."

"Oh sure," Clint said, "for a price, and usually at the cost of someone's life."

"I understand Tolliver and his deputies do what they have to do to get the job done," Kane said. "In my book that's all you can ask of a lawman, self-styled or otherwise."

"Who's putting up the money to pay them?" Clint asked.

"The town is," Kane said, "led by me."

"We voted on this, Adams," Burdette said. "The decision stands with those of us on the town council, the four of us, Judge Kelly, Reed Stephens, and the sheriff—although, of course, he doesn't sit on the council. We voted that if the sheriff decided it was necessary, he'd call Tolliver and his men in."

"Whose suggestion was it that Tolliver and his men be called in?"

"Why, the sheriff's."

"And what's your sheriff's name?" Clint asked. "I don't think I've seen him around since I came to town."

On the first day Clint had gone to the sheriff's office to check in with the man, but it had been locked up.

"He's been away," Burdette said, "but he got back last night, just in time for the trouble."

"His name," Wyatt said, "is Mark Randall."

"Randall?"

"You know him?" Burdette asked.

"I've heard the name," Clint said. "How long has he been sheriff here?"

"About six months."

"Any of you know what he did before that?"

The four men exchanged glances, and then Burdette said, "No. Do you?"

"He made his way with his gun," Clint said. "It wouldn't surprise me if he rode with Tolliver at one time."

"That's good," Kane said. "It means he knows Tolliver can get the job done."

It also meant, Clint thought, that he could steer some paying work Tolliver's way, even if the situation didn't quite call for Tolliver's brand of justice.

Suddenly, Clint had a bad taste in his mouth for these men.

"I think I'll call it a day, gents," he said, gathering up his money.

"So soon?" Kane asked. "It's still early." Most of the money Clint had won had come from the banker.

"You'll get your chance to get your money back tomorrow, Mr. Kane. I'll probably be around at least one more day."

He started to walk away from the table, then turned back and asked, "Anyone know when Tolliver and his men are due in town?"

"Thought I heard tomorrow," Kane said.

"Don't want to be around when he gets here, Adams?" Wyatt asked.

"On the contrary," Clint said. "I'm looking forward to seeing him and his men in action."

TWO

"I don't understand," Lydia Burdette said.

"What don't you understand, Lydia?" Clint asked.

They were in his bed at the hotel and had just finished making love. Both of their bodies were still covered with sweat.

"About this man—what's his name?"

"Who?" Clint asked, then realized that she must be talking about Tolliver. They had talked a little about him before they made love. If there was anything disconcerting about Lydia, it was that she could pick up a conversation from anywhere, even minutes or hours later.

"You mean Tolliver?"

"Yes, him. Why do you dislike him so much?"

"I don't know the man, so I can't dislike him, Lydia," Clint said, "but I know what I've heard."

6

"And you don't like what you've heard?"

"That's right."

"So why are you anxious to see him?" she asked with a puzzled frown.

"Because I don't like judging a man by his reputation," Clint said. "I don't like when it's done to me, so I don't like to do it to someone else. When he arrives in town, I'll be able to watch him and judge for myself."

"Well, I still don't understand," Lydia said. Another thing Clint had discovered about her was that she wasn't very bright. "All I care about is that you'll be staying a day or two more."

"Just out of curiosity."

"About Tolliver."

"Yes."

"I wish you was staying out of curiosity about me," she said, rolling over so that she was pressed against him, "but I guess I'll just have to take what I can get."

"Seems to me you've been getting an awful lot," he said, touching her.

"Not enough," she said, opening her mouth, "not nearly enough . . ."

Later, after Lydia left his room, Clint lay with his hands behind his head, staring at the ceiling. He'd been hearing about Dan Tolliver for the past couple of years, never paying much attention to the stories. All he knew for sure was that the man was never an official law enforcement officer of any kind. He'd heard that straight from the mouth of a genuine federal marshal, so he knew it was true.

He couldn't remember which of the poker players had said it, but they were right. Who was he to pass judgment on anyone? It had taken him years to get his reputation to the point it stood at today, where people didn't just arbitrarily consider him to be a cold-blooded killer. His reputation was now more that of a man who was extraordinarily good with a gun, who had a law enforcement past, as well as a somewhat shadowy past.

He got up and walked to the window to look down at the street. He was tired of playing poker with those same four men, and he was starting to notice more and more that Lydia was someone he just couldn't hold a conversation with. It was time to leave Ryland. Why then was he staying just to get a look at Dan Tolliver?

It was like he had told Lydia. It was curiosity, pure and simple. He wanted to see if Tolliver, like himself, was a man carrying around a reputation he hadn't quite earned, or if he actually was what people said he was—a sadistic killer who hid behind the "law"—even while he was not, in fact, a duly appointed lawman.

THREE

Dan Tolliver breathed on his badge again and wiped it vigorously until it shone brightly. It was late, and the saloon was about to close. Tomorrow he and his men would be in Ryland, Kansas, where their next job waited for them.

As he pinned the badge back onto his shirt, three of his men entered the saloon. His right-hand man, Carl Rhodes, was with them.

"Hey, boss," Rhodes said.

As the three men approached him, Tolliver noticed that their deputy badges did not shine as brightly as his own badge.

"Got time for a beer before we turn in?" Rhodes asked him.

"We've got a long ride ahead of us, Carl," Tolliver said coldly. "Take the men and get to bed."

9

Rhodes had had a few beers already that night—maybe a few more than a few, if Tolliver was any judge. He had been thinking for a while that Rhodes had been with him too long, was perhaps becoming too familiar. This incident might actually make up his mind for him.

"Come on, Carl," Frank Beckett said, grabbing for Rhodes's arm. "The others are in bed already, and we should be too."

Tolliver switched his gaze to Beckett. He was a young man, had been with the deputies the shortest time of all, and yet he seemed the one with the most sense, and the most smarts. If someone was going to replace Rhodes as top deputy, he might make a good choice. As the youngest, it would be interesting to see if he could make them toe the line.

"Listen to your young friend, Carl," Tolliver said. "Get off to bed."

The third man, Harry Chaplin, was just watching the proceedings with a worried frown.

"You, Chaplin," Tolliver said.

"Yes, sir?"

"No reason for you to stay here. Get to bed."

"Yes, sir."

"Aw, come on—" Rhodes added.

"Now!" Tolliver said.

Chaplin wasted no further time and got out of there, running for the hotel.

Tolliver stood up and faced the other two men. He was a tall man, at six three towering at least three inches above all of the other deputies save one. Gar Haywood was Tolliver's enforcer. He

was six five and seemingly built out of brick.
Haywood felt that he could defeat any man
alive hand-to-hand—except for Tolliver. The
first thing Tolliver had done when he signed
Haywood was whip him in front of all the other men. It was an impressive feat because, at
fifty-two, Tolliver was a full twenty years older
than the big black man. His hair was gray now,
but his jaw was still squared off and looked like
granite.

Now he stared down at Rhodes and said, "I
think it's time for a change, Carl."

"Wha—what change? Whataya talkin'
about?"

"I think you've been first deputy long
enough."

Rhodes continued to stare at Tolliver, as if
he couldn't understand the words he was hearing.

"What are you talkin' about, boss?"

"Beckett?"

"Yes, sir."

"You're first deputy now."

"Me?"

"That's right," Tolliver said. "Your first job is
to put this man to bed before he gets himself
into serious trouble."

Beckett hesitated only a second before saying, "Yes, sir. Right away. Come on, Carl."

"Hey, no, wait—" Rhodes said, but suddenly
his right arm was bent up behind his back
as Beckett took a firm hold on him. Beckett
was younger and larger than the five-foot-eight

Rhodes. He was not, however, stronger than Rhodes, so Tolliver found it interesting the way he used leverage against the stronger man.

"Let's go, Carl," Beckett said. "In the morning you'll be sober and able to understand what's going on. Right now you're only going to get yourself in deeper."

"Leggo—ow!"

"We'll see you in the morning, sir." Beckett, exerting more pressure, walked Carl Rhodes quickly out of the saloon.

Tolliver sat down. He liked what he saw in young Beckett. He thought that he had made the right decision—so far. It would take a while before Beckett proved himself completely, but he had handled his newfound authority quite well this first night.

Tolliver finished his beer under the weary eye of the bartender, who was waiting to close. Absently he touched the badge on his chest, smudging it with his thumb. He clucked his tongue at himself, pulled the badge off, and started cleaning it again.

The bartender heaved a sigh and rolled his eyes upward, but he wasn't about to actually say anything to Marshal Daniel Tolliver.

FOUR

In the morning Clint decided to go to the sheriff's office and meet Sheriff Mark Randall. Again, it was mostly out of curiosity. Randall had a reputation—there was that word again—as a competent man with a gun, a man who got the job done without anything fancy. Clint wondered how he had come to be sheriff of Ryland, Kansas.

Before breakfast he walked over to the lawman's office, but once again he found it closed and locked. Apparently Randall didn't have any deputies, and when he wasn't around, the office was locked. Clint decided he'd try again after breakfast.

Sheriff Mark Randall sat up and swung his feet to the floor of the jail cell. His back ached from sleeping on one of the jail

cots again. Whatever possessed him, he wondered, to run for sheriff of Ryland? At the
time it had seemed like a good idea. At
thirty-nine the man had been tired of wan-
dering around like a gypsy, picking up gun
work here and there. Riding with Tolliver's
Deputies, there had been a job, but he'd
had a falling-out with Carl Rhodes, Tolliver's
first deputy, and had gotten fired. He'd gone
right from that to this job, parlaying the fact
that he had been one of Tolliver's Deputies
into a landslide victory in the election for
the job.

Now, after six months, he was ready to move
on. That was what had given him the idea of
having the town hire Tolliver and his men to
clean out Roscoe Wills and his gang of rowdies.
Randall knew he could have done it himself,
but this would bring Tolliver to town and put
money in the man's pocket. After that maybe
Randall could get his job with Tolliver back.
He hoped so, because if he had to sleep on one
of these cots for another week, he'd be walking
stooped over for the rest of his life.

He stood up, stretched, and rubbed his stom-
ach as the morning hunger pains started.

Time for breakfast.

Clint had found a couple of places in town
that prepared a decent breakfast. Today he
chose the little café closest to the sheriff's
office. He was eating eggs and bacon when
a man wearing a badge walked in. As if to

make it even clearer, the waiter said, "Morning, Sheriff."

Speak of the devil, he thought—or more appropriately, think of him.

"Morning, Ed," Mark Randall said. "The usual."

"Steak and eggs comin' up," Ed said.

The waiter went into the kitchen, and Randall looked around the empty café and spotted Clint. Their eyes met for a long moment, and then Clint spoke.

"Sheriff Randall?"

"That's right."

Randall started to look around, trying to choose a table from all the empties.

"My name's Clint Adams."

"That's ni—what?" Randall turned and looked at him. "By God, it is you."

"Do you know me?"

"I seen you once, in Abilene, a long time ago," Randall said.

"Yeah," Clint said, "Abilene was a long time ago. Have a seat?"

"Huh?" Randall was obviously surprised at the invitation. "Sure, why not?"

He sat opposite Clint.

"When did you get into town?"

"About four days ago," Clint said. "I tried to check in with you, just to let you know I was here, but you weren't around."

"I was . . . busy."

"So I heard. Some trouble?"

"A little."

"I hear it's big enough for you to have talked the town council into hiring Dan Tolliver and his men."

Randall peered at Clint closely.

"You know Tolliver?"

"Not personally," Clint said, "just by reputation—same way I know you."

Randall looked surprised.

"You heard of me?"

"Once or twice."

"How—I mean, in what way?"

"Just as a man who got the job done," Clint said. "I have to tell you, I was surprised to find out that you were the sheriff here."

Randall smiled.

"I'm a little surprised myself."

"How'd it happen?" Clint asked. "Get tired of riding for Tolliver?"

"It wasn't that," Randall said, "it was—hey, wait. How did you know I rode with Tolliver?"

"Lucky guess," Clint said. "I guess you figure it won't hurt you to throw some business Tolliver's way, huh?"

"What's your interest?"

"Nothing," Clint said. "I'm just curious, that's all."

"Well . . . don't be so curious," Randall said, suddenly acting the part of sheriff to the hilt. "I don't have to explain my decisions to you."

"No, you don't, you surely don't," Clint said, "but you might have to explain to the town council that you had them hire Tolliver and his men when they weren't really needed."

"You want your breakfast here, Sheriff?" Ed asked, appearing at Randall's elbow.

"No, Ed," Randall said, looking away from Clint at the waiter. "Put it over—better yet, I'll take it to the office with me."

"I'll put it in a basket," Ed said.

Randall stood up and stared down at Clint.

"I appreciate you lettin' me know you're in town, Adams, but I don't appreciate bein' questioned by you. I'm the sheriff here, remember?"

"Oh, I remember, Sheriff," Clint said. "Don't worry. I just wonder how much longer you intend to hold on to the job."

"That ain't none of your business, is it?"

"No, it isn't," Clint agreed. "Like I told you before, I'm just curious."

"How much longer you intend to be in town?"

"At least until Tolliver gets here. I'm interested in getting a look at him."

Ed came out and handed the sheriff his breakfast basket.

"Well, just remember to try and control your curiosity while you're here—and don't start no trouble."

"My word of honor, Sheriff," Clint said. "I just want to see what's going on, that's all."

Randall stared at Clint, looking ridiculous standing there holding a wicker picnic basket, then he turned and walked out.

"Worse thing this town ever did," Ed said.

"What's that?"

"Vote that man in as sheriff."

"Why did they?"

"All that stuff about riding with Dan Tolliver, I guess," Ed said. "I didn't vote for him, though. I voted for the old sheriff, Pete Cummings."

"Jesus," Clint said, "I know Pete Cummings. He must be sixty by now."

"Sixty on the nose," Ed said. "I know because we was the same age."

"Where's Cummings now?"

"Gone. He left town when Randall beat him out for the job. Cummings was sheriff for seven years here. Town didn't show him no loyalty at all."

"They never do," Clint said.

"Worse thing this town ever did," Ed said again, then added, "and he don't even pay for his breakfast."

FIVE

When Clint woke the next morning he had a premonition. He thought that if he didn't leave town that day he was going to be sorry. He didn't have premonitions, as a rule. Considering the way this would turn out, though, he'd later wish he had paid heed to it. As it was he shrugged it off, wondering what harm it could do for him to stay around just long enough to meet Dan Tolliver and get a sense of what the man was like.

Just out of curiosity, of course.

He slid from the bed without waking Lydia, which was fairly easy since she slept very soundly. In fact, she slept more soundly than any woman he had ever known—and she snored. He figured to spend one more day in Ryland and then he was gone.

● ● ●

Clint was coming out of a restaurant after breakfast when he saw seven men riding down the main street of Ryland. There could be little doubt that they were Daniel Tolliver and his deputies. The sun glinted off the privately minted silver badges they were wearing.

One man was riding in the lead while the others fanned out behind him. Obviously this was Dan Tolliver. Clint studied him critically as the group came abreast of him. Tolliver was a tall man with steel-gray hair. His face was square-jawed, and his eyes met Clint's abruptly, as if he suddenly became aware of the fact that he was under scrutiny. The two men matched stares for a few seconds, and then Tolliver and his men were riding past. A couple of the men also looked over at Clint, who simply stared back. Clint was sure that he would be remembered later, right down to what he was wearing.

The six deputies were of varying sizes and ages, but they all wore the same expression on their faces—which was no expression at all. Just from Clint's short meeting with the sheriff, he could see Randall fitting right in. He wondered if Tolliver had room for another deputy on his staff.

Dan Tolliver studied the man on the board-walk, aware that the man was doing the same to him and had been for the past few minutes. There was something familiar about him, but Tolliver decided not to pursue it at the moment. If the man was truly interested in him, their paths would cross again. At that time Tolliver felt sure he'd be able to place the man.

He never forgot a face.

Clint had known bounty hunters before, some good, some bad, but he rarely knew them to ride in groups of more than two. Bounties just did not split well beyond a two-way split. Of course, Dan Tolliver would not call himself a bounty hunter, but Clint thought that would be a much more accurate label than lawman. From what he had heard of the way Tolliver worked, the deputies were on salaries and did not command equal shares of the "fee" that Tolliver charged for his services.

He watched as the seven men continued to ride until they were out of sight. No doubt they would stop at the livery first, and then a hotel. There were two hotels in town, but the one Clint was staying in was the largest. He decided to walk over there, pull up a chair in front, and see what developed.

SIX

Daniel Tolliver dismounted and his six deputies followed suit. He turned and handed the reins of his horse to the nearest man.

"Did you see him?" Spotted Dog asked.

Tolliver turned and looked at his ace tracker. Spotted Dog's white name was Tom Dees, but he preferred his Cherokee name. Half-Cherokee and half-white, he called himself full Cherokee and ignored the white blood that coursed through his veins.

"See who?" Frank Beckett asked.

Tolliver ignored Beckett and looked at Spotted Dog. If the Indian had been willing, Tolliver would have made him first deputy. But Spotted Dog didn't want any part of authority. All he wanted to do was track.

"I saw him."

"Saw who?" Beckett asked.

"Shut up, kid," Rhodes said. "Did you know him, Marshal?" Rhodes was intent on getting back the first deputy's position.

Tolliver didn't answer right away. The others watched him, waiting.

"There was something familiar about him," Marshal Tolliver finally said.

"What?" Beckett asked.

"Shut up, kid," Rhodes said. How could Tolliver have made him first deputy? The kid didn't know nothing!

"Don't tell me to shut up, Rhodes!" Beckett snapped. "I'm just askin'!"

Spotted Dog stared both of them into silence. The Cherokee was in his thirties, tall and sturdily built. There wasn't a white man alive who had ever seen him smile.

"When he sees him again," Spotted Dog said, "he will know him."

"Just takes twice," Rhodes said. "The marshal can put a name to a man the second time he sees him."

"That true?" Chaplin asked.

Spotted Dog and Rhodes both turned and stared at him, and the man subsided.

Harry Chaplin was holding the reins of Tolliver's horse so the marshal told the others, "Give your horses to Chaplin." He looked at the man and said, "Put them up and we'll see you at the hotel."

"Yessir."

"The rest of you come with me. We'll get situated at the hotel before we go and talk to the sheriff—what's his name again?"

"Randall," Rhodes offered anxiously.

Tolliver frowned.

"He rode with us, didn't he?"

"For about a year, Marshal," Rhodes said.

Tolliver thought a moment, then nodded.

"I remember him."

The others waited for him to say something else, but instead the marshal started walking. Spotted Dog fell in behind him and the others trailed after.

Rhodes trotted up next to Spotted Dog and asked, "Dog, did you know who that man was?"

Spotted Dog hesitated before answering.

"Tolliver will identify him."

"Then you do know, don't you?"

"He will remember."

"But sometimes he don't remember too good, does he, Dog?"

Spotted Dog looked at Rhodes and said, "Don't let the man hear you say that, Rhodes. He'd kill you."

"But it's true, ain't it?" Rhodes asked. "You and me been with him the longest, Dog. We seen him when he was sharp as could be, only lately he ain't been so sharp, has he?"

Spotted Dog looked ahead of him at the back of the man he'd been following and working with for over fifteen years, even before Rhodes and before Tolliver's Deputies.

Spotted Dog looked at Rhodes then and said, "He's just fine, Rhodes. Don't let me hear you say different, or I will kill you myself."

Rhodes flinched beneath Spotted Dog's look and said, "Sure, Dog . . . sure."

Spotted Dog lengthened his strides and moved away from Carl Rhodes. In point of fact he did recognize the man they had seen while riding into town. He knew that it was Clint Adams, the Gunsmith. Although he wondered what Adams was doing in town, he had no intention of bringing it up to Tolliver until the marshal recognized the man himself.

Spotted Dog knew better than anyone that Dan Tolliver was no longer the man he used to be. Over the past few years he had begun to forget things. He would have been making careless mistakes too, had Spotted Dog not been sticking so close to him that he was able to cover for the man—and he covered for him and protected him because he loved him. Tolliver had taken in Spotted Dog when nobody else would have him and let the tracker work for him. That had been fifteen years ago, and never once had Tolliver treated him like a half-breed.

Spotted Dog would allow no man to speak ill of Dan Tolliver—not and live.

SEVEN

Clint saw Tolliver and his men walking up the street toward the hotel. He counted six total, which meant one man had probably been left at the livery with the horses.

He saw Tolliver, and five other men spread out behind him, one of them black and almost six and a half feet tall. It was the man directly behind the self-styled marshal who drew his attention, though. He was tall and slender but strongly built. He appeared to be full-blooded Indian, but Clint knew for a fact that he was half-Cherokee and half-white. He'd heard stories about this man and knew that he was known as Spotted Dog. The Indian's reputation was as a tracker without peer. He looked quite capable of doing more than just tracking a man—and at the moment he was throwing hard looks at Clint as they drew closer.

26

Clint turned his gaze back to the head man, Tolliver. The marshal had his eyes on the hotel and wasn't looking at Clint at all.

The six men mounted the boardwalk and started toward the hotel entrance. For a moment Clint thought that Tolliver was going to walk right past him into the hotel, but the man stopped short. He still hadn't looked at Clint yet. The men behind him looked, but Tolliver continued to stare into the hotel lobby. Slowly, then, he turned his head and looked Clint in the eyes.

"Go on inside and register, boys," he said to his men. "Get me my own room, as usual."

"Right, Marshal," Rhodes said. "Come on, boys."

Rhodes and the others moved past Tolliver into the hotel lobby—all except for Spotted Dog, who remained solidly behind his boss.

"You're Clint Adams, right?" Tolliver asked.

"That's right," Clint said. "I'm impressed. Have we met?"

"No, no," Tolliver said, "but I know your reputation, of course."

"You recognized me from my reputation?"

Tolliver almost smiled, but not quite.

"No, of course not. I saw you once . . . or was it twice?" Tolliver frowned, and Clint saw indecisiveness in the man's eyes. "Spotted Dog?"

"Twice," the half-breed said.

Suddenly, Tolliver's eyes cleared and he looked confident again. Clint couldn't help feeling that a lot of the man's confidence was being carried by the Indian.

"That's right, twice," Tolliver said. "I don't recall exactly where, at the moment, but it's not important."

"No," Clint said, "it's not."

"Are you in town on any kind of . . . business?" Tolliver asked.

"No," Clint said, "no business. I'm just passing through."

"Well then," Tolliver said, "maybe we can have a drink later."

"Sure," Clint said, "why not?"

Tolliver nodded, started into the hotel, and then stopped again.

"Do you know the sheriff here?"

"I've met him," Clint said.

"What do you think of him?"

"Not much," Clint said, "but then, I'd think you'd know more about him than I would."

"Why is that?" Tolliver asked, with a frown.

"You knew him," Clint said.

Tolliver continued to frown.

"He rode with you."

"Randall," Spotted Dog said.

"Hmm?" Tolliver said. "Oh, yes. Uh, this is Spotted Dog."

"Yes," Clint said, "I've heard of him."

"Reputations," Tolliver said.

"His is impressive," Clint said. "They say he can track anything, human or animal."

"Reputations," Tolliver said. "We know how blown up they can be."

"Oh, yes." Clint Adams knew that very well.

"You must know that better than most," Tolliver said, as if reading Clint's mind.

"Yes."

"Well," Tolliver said, "in Spotted Dog's case, his reputation is not blown up enough."

"I see."

"We'll have that drink later," Tolliver said.

"Sure," Clint said. "Anytime."

Tolliver looked over his shoulder at Spotted Dog, then went into the lobby with the Cherokee half-breed following him.

No, Clint thought, he's doing more than just following him, he's covering his back, just as he's probably been doing for years.

Clint sat back and pondered his first meeting with Dan Tolliver. It was plain to him that the man was having some problems with his memory. He didn't know if that was the result of an injury, or simply age. Tolliver looked to be in his fifties but could have been older. Maybe his mind was just fogging from age. Whatever the reason, though, he shouldn't have been leading six "deputies" into battle—for want of a better way of putting it.

Of course, that was just Clint's opinion. He wondered if anyone else would notice what he did, that Tolliver had some problem remembering things, that Spotted Dog was there to help him when he did. Would anyone who had hired the man even care enough to notice?

Probably not.

EIGHT

Spotted Dog walked Dan Tolliver to his room, where they dropped off the marshal's gear.

"Time for a nap," the Cherokee said.

If anyone had seen the two men when they were alone, they would not have believed the difference in the relationship.

Tolliver did not argue. He sat down on the bed, and Spotted Dog crouched down in front of him and started removing his boots.

"Make sure the others are settled in, Dog," Tolliver said.

"I will."

"Watch young Beckett," Tolliver said, as Spotted Dog swung his legs up onto the bed. While the man was lying there, the Indian loosened his gun belt and slid it from beneath him.

"And watch Rhodes," Tolliver said sleepily. "He thinks I don't see what he's doing. He

wants the first deputy job back, but he's not
going to get it."

"All right."

"I really wish you'd take the job, Dog."

"No."

"I know, I know," Tolliver mumbled, "you
don't want it, but it would really be . . . a . . .
help. . . ."

Spotted Dog stood staring down at the older
man, wondering how much longer he'd be able
to hold everything together. Not only did he
have to keep people from realizing what was
happening to Tolliver, but he had to keep the
man himself from seeing it.

He thought about Clint Adams. The man
was all eyes, noticing everything. He was sure
that Adams had caught on. Also, Carl Rhodes.
The man had been riding with Tolliver for a
long time, something Spotted Dog just did not
understand. Rhodes was not, in the Indian's
eyes, a good man. He couldn't understand it
when Tolliver had made Rhodes first deputy.
It made more sense now that the man had been
replaced, but how much sense did it make to
give the job to a young man like Beckett? Then
again, Spotted Dog had turned the job down so
often, who was he to judge who Tolliver chose
for the job?

The older man's breathing was even, regu-
lar, as he slept. Spotted Dog slipped from the
room without waking Tolliver. He hoped Clint
Adams was still in front of the hotel.

NINE

Clint was surprised when Spotted Dog came out of the hotel so soon after entering.

"I am glad you are still here," the Indian said.

"Is that a fact?"

"Let's take a walk."

Clint just stared up at the man.

Spotted Dog rephrased the statement.

"Will you take a walk with me?"

"Why?"

"I need to talk to you."

Clint hesitated a moment, then shrugged and stood up. Side by side, the two men began to walk down the street.

"What's on your mind?" Clint asked.

"Marshal Tolliver."

"Marshal?" Clint said. "That's just what he

calls himself, Spotted Dog. Let's not get confused—"

Spotted Dog held up his hand.

"I don't want to argue about what he calls himself," he said.

"What do you want to argue about?"

"I do not want to argue," the Indian said. "I want to talk."

"So you said, but you haven't started yet."

"I want to know why you are here."

"I told Tolliver, I'm just passing through."

"A coincidence, then?"

Well, Clint thought, not really. After all, he would have been gone already except he had heard Tolliver was coming to town and wanted to meet him. Should he tell that to Spotted Dog?

"That's right," he said, even though he didn't believe in coincidences himself.

"Then you will be leaving."

"Yes."

"Soon?"

Clint hesitated, then said, "Soon enough."

Spotted Dog stopped short, turning to face Clint.

"I would like you to leave today, or tomorrow."

"Is that a fact?"

"Yes."

"Why?"

Spotted Dog didn't answer.

"Why are you protecting him?"

"I work for him."

"No, I don't mean that kind of protection," Clint said. "Not just watching his back. I mean why are you covering up for him?"

Spotted Dog looked away.

"I don't know what you mean."

"Sure you do," Clint said. "He's losing it, isn't he? Starting to have memory lapses, and lapses in judgment?"

"That is ridiculous," Spotted Dog said. "He is Dan Tolliver—"

"Sure he is, but he's not the Dan Tolliver he used to be. There's no shame in it, Spotted Dog. None of us is the man he used to be."

"He is."

"You want him to be."

"No!" Spotted Dog was vehement now, so much so that a man and woman who were passing turned to look. The Indian glared at them and they hurried away.

"You will leave town," Spotted Dog said to Clint.

"I'll leave when I'm ready," Clint said. "Besides, Tolliver said he wanted to have a drink with me. If I left now it would be rude."

"Do not force me to . . ."

"To what, Spotted Dog?" Clint asked. He'd noticed earlier that Spotted Dog did not wear a gun. All he had on his belt was a knife— granted it was a formidable knife, but it still would not be able to go up against a gun. "You going to force me to leave? How?"

"I will warn you one time," Spotted Dog said. "Do not try to hurt him."

"Why would I do that?"

"Just remember," Spotted Dog said, and walked away.

TEN

After talking to Spotted Dog, Clint decided to try to find out exactly what the big problem was that had brought Tolliver and his deputies to town.

He doubted that Sheriff Randall would talk to him, but he thought he knew someone who would. He walked over to the general store.

Lydia and her father were there working, and she saw him as he entered the store.

"Hello, Clint." She smiled brightly at him. As far as they knew, her father still didn't suspect that anything was going on between them, and Clint wanted to keep it that way. "Can I help you get anything?"

"I'll be leaving in a day or two," he said, "and I'll need to outfit myself."

She averted her face so that her father

36

couldn't see and thrust out her bottom lip in a pout.

"Let me help you," she said, coming out from behind the counter.

They walked to a corner of the store where her father couldn't hear what they were saying.

"When are you leaving?" she asked. "Tomorrow?"

He thought about Spotted Dog's demand that he leave tomorrow and said, "No, definitely not."

"The day after?"

"Maybe."

"Then we have another night," she said, smiling.

"Lydia, I'm curious about something."

"Really?" she asked. "There's something you still don't know after the past few nights?"

"No, not about that," he said. "Something else."

"Then what?"

"Your father's on the town council."

"So?"

"I'd like to find out why the council approved the hiring of Dan Tolliver and his deputies."

"That's what you're curious about?" She looked disappointed.

"Yes."

"Well, I can answer that for you."

"You can?"

"Sure," she said. "I eavesdrop all the time when one of the other council members comes over."

"Then what is it?"

"Roscoe Wills."

"Who?"

"Roscoe Wills? Oh, I forgot, you haven't been here long enough to know about Roscoe and his gang."

"What about them?"

"They're causing trouble."

"What kind of trouble?"

"Oh, vandalism, some robberies—"

"Anybody hurt?"

"Oh, no," she said, "Roscoe wouldn't hurt anybody."

"You know him well?"

"We grew up together," she said, "him and the others."

"The others in his gang?"

"That's right."

"How many are there?"

"Four."

"And they're all your age?"

"More or less."

"Are they dangerous enough to warrant hiring Tolliver and his men?"

"I didn't think so," she said, "but the sheriff seemed to, and the town council went along with it." She laughed. "Roscoe's always been high-spirited."

Clint frowned. He couldn't understand why they'd call in a man like "Marshal" Dan Tolliver just for four high-spirited young men. Something wasn't right here.

"Thanks, Lydia."

"What about your supplies?" she asked. "Don't you want them?"

"I'll pick them up another day."

"What about me?" she asked coyly. "Will you pick me up another day too?"

"I'll see you later," he said.

"Promise?"

Suddenly, he was annoyed.

"No, I don't promise, Lydia," he said testily. "I might have something else to do tonight. We'll see what happens with the rest of the day, okay?"

"Okay," she said, backing off a bit, "you don't have to bite my head off."

Instantly he was sorry, and he apologized to her, taking her hands.

"I'll see you later," he added, "more than likely."

"Sure," she said.

She went back to her counter, and he went outside.

He didn't know who Roscoe Wills was, but Dan Tolliver and his men usually left a lot of dead bodies behind them.

Clint fervently hoped that this would not be the case this time. It would be a shame if those young men were killed just because Sheriff Randall wanted to throw some work Tolliver's way, as a way to get back into Tolliver's Deputies.

ELEVEN

Clint went from the general store to Sheriff Randall's office. It was not locked this time, and he entered without knocking. Randall looked up from his desk and frowned when he saw who it was.

"What do you want?" he asked.

"Tolliver and his men are in town."

"I heard," Randall said, "but he ain't been to see me yet."

"He will be," Clint said. "You've got to call him off, Randall."

"What?"

"Roscoe Wills doesn't sound like the kind of man you'd need Dan Tolliver for."

"What do you know about Roscoe Wills?"

"Not much, but—"

"Then don't try to tell me my job, Adams," Randall said. His heart was pounding, but he

40

knew he couldn't back down from anyone, not even the Gunsmith. That would look bad for Tolliver, and he'd never take him on again. "Roscoe and his gang are dangerous, and I ain't about to go up against them myself. I need Tolliver."

"You need Tolliver to get you out of this town," Clint said. "Why does he have to kill four young men before you can leave?"

"Nobody knows if he's gonna kill anybody," Randall said.

"What do you think he's going to do?" Clint asked. "Ask them politely to leave?"

"I don't know what he's gonna do," Randall said. "I don't try to tell him his job, and you shouldn't try to tell me mine."

"I'm telling you that four young men are going to be killed for no reason. Will you be able to live with that if it happens?"

"If it happens, it'll be their own doing, not mine," Randall said. "I ain't gonna lose sleep over no four lawbreakers."

Clint stared at Randall for a few seconds and then asked, "Do you want to ride with Dan Tolliver again that badly? Is this the only way you can think of doing it?"

"What do you care?" Randall asked. "What's your interest, anyway?"

"I just don't want to see unnecessary blood-shed," Clint said.

"Come on, Adams," Randall said. "With your reputation? You ain't afraid of a little blood. Come on, what's your angle?"

"I don't have an angle, Randall," Clint said. "I already told you my interest."

"Why don't you just move on, Adams? Tonight, even. Just leave town. There's nothing going on here that's any of your business."

"I wonder why so many people want me out of town," Clint said.

"Oh yeah? Who besides me?"

"Spotted Dog."

Randall stiffened at the sound of the Indian's name.

"I see you remember Spotted Dog. I think maybe you're even afraid of him."

"Dog and I know each other," Randall said uncomfortably.

"Why would you want to ride with him, then?" Clint asked.

Randall stared at Clint for a moment, then seemed to make a decision. Maybe he figured they were alone, and he could always deny anything he said.

"I never had any family, Adams," he said, "and I never in my life had money . . . except when I rode with Tolliver and his deputies."

"So why did you stop riding with them?"

Randall opened his mouth, as if to answer, then thought better of it.

"Never mind," he said. "That's none of your business. Just do yourself a favor and stay out of the way when the action starts."

"Oh, don't worry," Clint said. "I don't intend to get in the way."

"Good."

"I just might stick around to see what happens, though," Clint said. "There may be some need for a reliable witness later. Who knows?"

With that he left the office, slamming the door behind him.

Randall sat at his desk after Clint Adams left, waiting for his heart to return to beating normally. It was bad enough he was afraid of Adams, the mention of Spotted Dog had spooked him badly. The half-breed scared the shit out of him. When they rode together they had gotten on well enough, but there was something about the quiet tracker that just made Randall uneasy.

He'd been hoping that Spotted Dog wouldn't be with Tolliver, but that was a futile hope from the beginning. If he wanted to ride with Tolliver again, that meant he was going to have to deal with Spotted Dog. Just like he tried to do with Adams, he was going to have to hide the fact that the Indian scared him.

TWELVE

From the jail Clint returned to the general
store. He didn't see Lydia, but her father was
behind the counter.

"Mr. Burdette, where's Lydia?"

Burdette frowned at him.

"She's in the back," he said, "Why?"

"I need to speak with her."

"She's working, Adams," he said. "Are you
going to play poker tonight?"

"I don't know," Clint said. "I really need to
speak with Lydia."

"I told you, she's work—"

"I need to ask her one question."

Burdette frowned even more.

"About what?"

"Roscoe Wells?"

"That shiftless son of a bitch?" Burdette said,
with feeling. "I've warned him and his kind

44

to stay away from my daughter. She's a good girl."

"I'm sure she is, Mr. Burdette."

"What makes you think she'd know where he is?" Burdette demanded.

"Well, sir . . . they seem to be about the same age. I figured there was no harm in asking."

"What do you want with Wells?"

"I just want to talk to him."

"Well, you better talk fast."

"Why is that?"

"Because Dan Tolliver and his men are coming to town to get rid of him, that's why," Burdette said, very pleased. "Roscoe Wells and his kind won't be causing trouble in this town ever again."

"Please, Mr. Burdette," Clint said, "I won't keep her. Just one—"

"Oh, all right, then," Burdette said. "She's in the storeroom."

"Thanks."

"Sure wish you'd play poker tonight," Burdette said. "Give us a chance to get some of our money back."

"I'll sure try, Mr. Burdette."

He went around the counter into the storeroom and found Lydia, apparently taking inventory of some stock.

"Lydia—"

She turned quickly and her eyes widened.

"Clint, how did you get back here?"

"I asked your father if I could talk to you."

She smiled.

"Come to apologize?"

"I thought I did that before."

"Not enough," she said, "not nearly enough."

"Lydia," he said, "I want to find Roscoe Wells."

"So?"

"Do you know where he is?"

"I might."

"Well, either you do or you don't."

"I might," she said, her hand playing with the bodice of her dress.

She wanted to play.

"What do you want?" he asked.

"I want you to apologize."

"I'm sorry—"

"No," she said, "not like that. I want you to really apologize."

Her hands went behind her, and she undid her dress. It started to fall down her arms.

"Lydia, your father is right out front!"

"Then it better be a quiet apology," she said, letting her dress drop to the floor. She stood naked in the center of the storeroom, where her father could walk in anytime and catch them.

Suddenly, Clint had an erection.

"Lydia . . ." he said thickly.

"Shh," she said, putting her forefinger to her lips. "Quietly, I said."

He went to her, took her in his arms, and kissed her. She pressed her hot body to him, and he could feel her heat right through his clothes. She undid his belt and his pants and started pushing them down his thighs. He lifted her up onto a barrel, and she spread her legs. He reached between her legs, wanting to touch her, to get her wet, but she was plenty wet enough already.

"Come on, come on . . ." she urged him, her mouth pressed to his ear.

He kissed her again, on the mouth, the shoulders, and then got on his knees so he could kiss her breasts and suck her nipples. She put her hands on his shoulders then and exerted pressure, pushing him still lower. When his face was between her legs, she pushed on his shoulders, lifting herself just a bit, and he began to lick and suck her where she was deliciously wet and sticky. . . .

With his pants still around his ankles, he stood and slid his hands beneath her, cupping her buttocks, and entered her. A cry of pleasure caught in her throat, and she bit him on the shoulder in an attempt to stifle further cries as he drove into her.

This was the most interesting his relationship with Lydia had been up till now.

She slid her arms around him, and her legs, and held tightly. He staggered back, pulling her off the barrel and taking her weight. He almost tripped over his pants, in which case they would have fallen to the floor noisily, but he righted himself and she began to ride him, both hands clasped behind his neck, moving her weight up and down on him, grunting with the effort. If her father walked in now and took it into his mind to shoot him, Clint knew he'd be a dead man.

But what a way to die. . . .

While Clint dressed in the storeroom, Lydia remained naked, sitting on the barrel. As he started to leave the room she stared at him and slid her hand down between her legs, touching herself. Goddamned if he wasn't rigid and hard again.

"Tonight," he said to her. "My room."

"Maybe," she said with a lewd smile. "I'll have to see. I may be doing something else."

He guessed he deserved that.

He left the room with the taste of her still on his tongue, the scent of her on his fingers and face. . . .

"I thought you said you wouldn't be long," Burdette said, staring at him strangely. "My girl's got a lot of work, you know."

"I know, sir. I'm sorry."

"Did she know where to find him?"

"Actually, no, she didn't."

"Then what took so long?"

"She, uh, needed some help moving some barrels."

"Barrels?"

"Yes, there was, uh, one in particular she had some problem with."

"Ah," Burdette said, "that's why I wish I'd had a son. No boy of mine would have needed help moving a barrel."

Clint stared at Burdette for a few moments, then said, "If you don't mind me saying so, Burdette, that's a pretty stupid thing to say."

"Who asked you?"

"Nobody, I guess" Clint said, "but I'm telling you, anyway. You've got yourself a fine daughter there. Give her a chance."

Clint left, armed with a couple of places Roscoe Wells might be. As he walked out, though, he found himself feeling sorry for Lydia Burdette, and liking her a whole lot more than ever before.

THIRTEEN

The first place Lydia told Clint Roscoe Wells might be was a small shack just north of town. She had to give him specific directions how to get there, because it was not in plain sight.

"It's hidden behind a stand of trees and a cluster of rocks," she told him. "Whoever built it wanted a place where they'd never be found."

"How did Wells find it?" Clint asked.

"He and I found it when we were twelve," she said. "We used it as a place to be . . . alone."

"At twelve?" he asked.

"So it took me a little longer than most girls," she said with a playful smile.

It was well hidden, all right, so well hidden that Clint passed it twice before he finally found it. Instead of approaching on horseback, he dismounted and left Duke about a hundred yards away. He didn't want anybody taking a hasty shot at him while he rode up.

He approached on foot, wondering if Roscoe Wells and his "gang" were inside. Lydia had laughed when he'd called Roscoe and his friends a gang.

"What's a gang?" she asked. "They're just a bunch of boys having some fun."

"They're not boys, Lydia," he said, "they're men."

"They don't act like men," she said. "They're so . . . young."

"They're your age."

She made a face.

"When we were twelve they were my age, but once we hit fifteen I started to pull ahead of them. Now they just seem silly." She gave him another of her special lewd looks and added, "I prefer men!"

As he got closer to the shack, the door opened and a man stepped out. He looked to be the same age as Lydia Burdette.

"Don't come no closer," the man said.

"I'm looking for Roscoe Wells."

"Well," the man said, his thumbs hooked into his gun belt, "why don't you turn around and just keep on looking."

"A friend of his told me I might find him here."

The man frowned.

"What friend?"

"Lydia Burdette."

"Lydia sent you here?"

"Yes," Clint said, "and she told me how to find the place. I still passed it twice, though."

"It's a hard place to find, all right," the man said, and then he realized that he had dropped his hardcase act and squared his shoulders. "What do you want with Roscoe, Mister?"

"I just want to talk to him."

"About what?"

"About saving his life."

The man's eyes popped and suddenly he looked years younger.

"Huh?"

"Do you think that's an interesting subject?"

"I guess so."

"So where is he?"

"He ain't—" the man started to say, but before he could finish, the door opened again and another man stepped out.

"What's your name?" the man asked.

"Clint Adams."

Both men gaped at him.

"You mean, the Gunsmith?" the first man asked.

"That's right."

"Jeez . . ." he said, looking at the second man.

"I'm Roscoe Wells," the second man said. "Why don't you come on inside?"

FOURTEEN

Clint stepped inside the shack and found that, other than he and the two men, it was empty.

"I understood there were four of you," he said.

"There are," Roscoe Wells said. "The others are . . . away."

"What do you want?" the other man asked.

"Quiet, Ray," Wells said. He looked at Clint and asked, "What do you want? What was that stuff about saving my life?"

"Dan Tolliver is in town."

"So?"

"Do you know who he is?"

Wells shrugged.

"Sure."

"Then you know why he's here."

"Why?"

"For you."

Wells and Ray exchanged a glance.

"Why would he be here for us?" Ray asked. "We ain't outlaws."

"Maybe not," Clint said, "but you're a pain in the butt to somebody."

Wells laughed.

"Almost everybody."

"Well, the sheriff proposed bringing in Tolliver and his men, and the town council approved it. They all arrived here today. Before long they'll probably come looking for you."

Again the two younger men exchanged a glance.

"Let 'em," Wells said. "Tolliver's been around a long time. He's an old man."

"The men with him aren't so old."

"We can take care of them," Wells said.

"Roscoe," Ray said, "I don't know—"

"Quiet, Ray!" He looked at Clint, his arms folded across his chest. "Is that all you came out here about?"

Clint looked at the well-worn Colts each man had in equally worn holsters.

"You boys know how to use those guns?" he asked.

"We know how," Roscoe Wells said. "Don't you worry about us, Mr. Gunsmith. You ain't the only one who can shoot."

"I know," Clint said, "believe me, I know. Now look, boys—"

"Don't call us boys!" Wells snapped.

"Then don't act like boys," Clint replied. "You

can't hope to go up against Tolliver and his deputies and come out alive. It just isn't going to happen."

"You don't think so?" Wells asked, thrusting his jaw out. "You just watch us."

"Hey, Roscoe, maybe he's—"

"Damn it, Ray," Wells said, turning on his friend quickly, "I told you to shut up!"

"Why don't you let him talk?" Clint asked.

"Because he don't ever have nothing smart to say," Wells said, "that's why."

Ray stood staring at Wells's back for a few moments, then turned and stalked out of the shack.

"Now look what you did," Wells said. "What did you come out here for?"

"To try and keep you from getting killed," Clint said. "I told you that."

"Why? You don't know me."

"I don't want to see you or your friends getting killed—or anybody getting killed—just because you're a little wild."

"We ain't wild," Wells said, "we're bad, we're real bad. We're a gang!"

"Sure you are," Clint said. "Take my advice, Roscoe. Talk to your friends and see what they want to do. Don't make any rash decisions that are going to cost them their lives."

"I make all the decisions in this gang, Mr. Gunsmith," Wells said. "They'll do what I tell them."

"For their sake," Clint said, "I hope you're wrong."

"Why don't you get out of here?" Wells shouted. "And don't be coming back here to look for us, because we won't be here anymore."

"I was just trying to help," Clint said, and left.

When he got back to his horse, he found the other man, Ray, waiting there.

"Was all that true?"

"All what?"

"About Tolliver comin' to get us."

"It was true," Clint said. "Why would I lie? Roscoe's going to get you and your friends killed, Ray."

"What am I supposed to do?"

"Talk to them," Clint said. "Don't let them follow him. Maybe he'll listen to reason if you all side against him."

"You don't know Roscoe," Ray said, shaking his head. "He'll just get more bullheaded."

"It's worth a try, Ray," Clint said. "Think about it."

"I will, Mr. Adams."

"I hope you can talk some sense into him."

Clint mounted up and rode back to town, thinking that he had done all he could do—almost.

FIFTEEN

When the door to Sheriff Mark Randall's office opened he looked up, expecting to see Clint Adams again. Instead he was looking at a man he hadn't seen in over six months.

Spotted Dog.

"Hello, Dog."

Spotted Dog didn't reply; he just walked across the room and stood in front of Randall's desk.

"What is Clint Adams doing here?"

Randall shrugged, keeping both hands on the top of the desk.

"He's just passin' through, Dog."

"Make him leave."

"I tried."

"Why?"

"He, uh, suddenly has taken an interest in

what you and Da—I mean, the marshal are doin' here."

"You are the law," Spotted Dog said. "Make him leave."

"I told you, I tried, Dog," Randall said. "He won't go. I can't stand up to his gun, you know that."

"If he gets in our way, he will be sorry," Spotted Dog said.

"I know."

"And so will you."

Randall swallowed hard and moistened his mouth, but by the time he thought he could speak, Spotted Dog was gone.

"Damn!"

When Dan Tolliver woke, he looked for Spotted Dog but couldn't find him. He went to another room and found Frank Beckett.

"You seen Spotted Dog, Beckett?"

"No, sir," Beckett said. "Not since we first got to town."

"Hmm," Tolliver said. "Where are the other boys?"

"They're at the saloon."

"How many saloons this town got?"

"Two," Beckett said.

"You checked out the town?"

"Yes, sir."

Tolliver nodded and thought a moment before speaking again.

"All right, I have a job for you, Beckett."

•   •   •

When Clint got back to his hotel, he headed
for the stairs but stopped when he heard his
name.

"Clint Adams?"

He turned and saw a man approaching him.
He was barely older than Roscoe Wells.

"Yes?"

He recognized him then as one of the men
who had ridden in with Tolliver.

"My name is Frank Beckett," the man said.
"I rode in with Marshal Tolliver."

"I remember. What can I do for you?"

"The marshal wanted me to wait here for
you and invite you to have a drink with him
over at the saloon."

"Is he there now?"

"Yes, he is."

"All right, then," Clint said, "lead the way.
We wouldn't want to keep the marshal waiting, now would we?"

"No, sir."

They left the hotel with Beckett in the lead
and headed for one of Ryland's two saloons.

Spotted Dog saw Clint and Beckett walking
down the street and hurriedly fell in behind
them. He was afraid the marshal had awakened
sooner than expected. He did not want anyone—especially Clint Adams—talking to Dan
Tolliver when he was not around.

He caught up to them and asked Beckett,
"Where are you going?"

Beckett turned in surprise.

"Oh, the marshal wants me to bring Mr. Adams to the Crossland Saloon."

"I'll do it," Spotted Dog said.

Beckett frowned.

"I'm first deputy, Spotted Dog, and—"

"I said I will do it!"

All three men stopped short, and Spotted Dog and Beckett faced each other. For a moment Clint thought the younger man would stand up to the Indian, but in the end he averted his eyes and took a step back.

"Well, okay," he said, "I guess as long as he gets there . . ."

"I will explain it to the marshal," Spotted Dog said. He looked at Clint and said, "Come."

As they walked away from Beckett, Clint said, "That kid is first deputy?"

Spotted Dog didn't answer. Clint Adams's tone clearly implied that here was another example of Tolliver's fading judgment.

SIXTEEN

When Clint and Spotted Dog entered the saloon, Clint spotted Dan Tolliver right away. It was easy. He was sitting on one side of the room and the other patrons were seated on the other. It was as if they had cleared that side of the room for him purposely.

Tolliver had a beer in front of him and was staring into it intently. Spotted Dog and Clint walked over to his table, but the man did not look up at them. Clint looked at Spotted Dog, who made a concerted effort not to return the look.

"Marshal," the Indian said.

No answer.

Spotted Dog moved around behind the man's chair.

"Marshal?"

"Hmm?" Tolliver started, then looked up at

61

Spotted Dog. "Dog, where did you come from?"

"Clint Adams is here, Marshal."

"He is?" Tolliver looked around and saw Clint. "Ah, Adams, have a seat."

"Thank you."

Tolliver looked at Spotted Dog again.

"I asked Beckett to bring Adams here," he said. "I couldn't find you."

"I was . . . out."

"Obviously," Tolliver said. "In the future, Dog, I'd appreciate it if you wouldn't be changin' my orders, huh? Understand?"

Spotted Dog hesitated a second and then said, "Yes, sir."

"Okay, now get Adams a beer, huh?"

"I will have the bartender bring it."

"No, Dog," Tolliver said, looking up at the man, "I told you to bring it."

Clint saw Spotted Dog's jaw muscles tighten, but the Indian nodded.

"As you wish."

Tolliver watched as Spotted Dog walked to the bar to get the beer.

"He's been with me a long time," he said, "but every so often I got to kick him in the butt, you know?"

"He seems very loyal."

"He is, he is," Tolliver said, looking at Clint. "I'd make him my first deputy if he'd take the goddamn job. Since he don't, I rag him sometimes, like now. Watch."

Spotted Dog came back and set a beer mug down in front of Clint.

"If you was my first deputy I wouldn't make you fetch beer," Tolliver said.

Spotted Dog gave Tolliver a heavy-lidded look and then said, "I'll sit at another table and wait."

With that the Indian went to the next table and sat down alone, without a drink.

"He don't rag worth a shit," Tolliver said, "and I ain't never seen him take a drink. You suppose that stuff about Indians not bein' able to handle liquor is true?"

"I don't know," Clint said. "Maybe it's just that Indians don't get very much of it, so when they do they can't handle it."

"Maybe," Tolliver said, "maybe you're right."

"Did you invite me for a drink to ask what I thought about Indians and whiskey?"

"No, no," Tolliver said, "course not."

Clint noticed that the man's speech patterns had changed. Earlier, when they'd first met, he'd sounded educated, and now he sounded like some uneducated good ol' boy from the mountains. Add in all that talk about Indians drinking whiskey, and Clint was convinced that Tolliver was on the verge of losing it completely.

Apparently, though, he still ran the show. Clint decided that this might work to his advantage. Maybe he'd be able to talk the man out of going after Roscoe Wills and his "gang."

SEVENTEEN

"What did you want to talk to me about?" Clint asked.

"Well, sir, I wanted to offer you a job," Tolliver said.

Clint couldn't believe his ears.

"As one of your deputies?"

"No, not just as one of my deputies," Tolliver said, "as my first deputy."

"What about the first deputy you have now?"

"He's a kid," Tolliver said. "I'll just drop him down a peg."

"What about Spotted Dog?"

"He don't want the job."

"Did you tell him you were going to offer it to me?" Clint asked.

"No."

"What do you suppose he'd think about it?"

"He works for me," Tolliver said. "He thinks

what I tell him to think."

All of a sudden the old Dan Tolliver—or what Clint assumed was the old Tolliver—was back. His eyes were bright and clear, and he was determined and confident. How long did the spells of absolute lucidity last? Clint wondered. Or were his confused moments the spells?

"I don't think so," Clint said.

"You haven't heard my offer yet."

"It really doesn't matter," Clint said. "I wouldn't accept."

"Are you telling me you wouldn't accept any amount of money to ride with me?"

"That's right."

Tolliver straightened his back, puffed out his chest, and stared back at Clint hard.

"Why not?" he demanded. "Are you too good to ride with Dan Tolliver? You think because you got a big rep as some kind of legend—"

"My reason is very simple," Clint said, cutting the man off.

"What?"

"I don't approve of what you do," Clint said. "I would no sooner ride with you than I would with a group of bounty hunters."

"I am not a bounty hunter, sir."

"Aren't you, Tolliver?" Clint asked. "Don't you take money to hunt people down and, in some cases, kill them?"

"I take money to uphold the law," Tolliver said, "like any sheriff or U.S. marshal does."

"But you're not a sheriff, or a U.S. marshal," Clint said. "That badge on your chest was not pinned there by any federal official. You bought and paid for it yourself and pinned it on yourself."

"I uphold the law."

"It's not your job."

"If more people whose job it wasn't did it, we'd have a better country."

"Maybe," Clint said, "and maybe not." He didn't want to get on the subject of vigilantism. That was something else he didn't approve of.

"You seem to have high morals for a man with your reputation."

"You and I both know what reputations are worth, Tolliver."

"I don't know about you," Tolliver said, "but mine's been earned."

"With blood."

"Sometimes, yes, when the need was there. Don't tell me you haven't killed half the men you've been credited with killing?"

"I haven't been keeping a tally." Clint decided to approach his subject, even though in Tolliver's present state he might not be receptive. "I want to talk to you about your job here."

"What of it?" Tolliver asked. "What's your interest?"

"I just don't want to see any unnecessary bloodshed," Clint said.

"I see," Tolliver said coldly. "Another moral issue."

"If it's a moral issue to want to stop senseless killing, then yes."

"Say your piece," Tolliver said, "I have things to attend to."

"The men you've been brought here to . . . handle," Clint began.

"What about them?"

"They don't warrant your presence," Clint said. "They're not outlaws, they're not gunmen, they're just a thorn in someone's side."

"Yes," Tolliver said, "the town's."

"Tolliver," Clint said, "I'm telling you that there's no need to kill them."

"I will be the judge of that," Tolliver said. "Regardless of what you think, Adams, I don't just ride into town and start shooting. I look into the situation, evaluate it, and then proceed accordingly."

"I see."

"That's what I'll do here," Tolliver said. "So you see, there's really no need for you to, uh, try to help me?"

"I wasn't trying to help you," Clint said candidly. "I was trying to help the four young men you've been brought here to . . . to what?"

"As you said before," Tolliver reminded him, "I've been brought here to handle a situation, and that is what I will do."

Clint stared across the table at the man. In Tolliver's present state of mind Clint could almost believe that the man's reputation as a killer was exaggerated—except that he himself claimed to have earned his rep.

"Is there anything else I can help you with?" Tolliver asked.

"No," Clint said, "I think that about covers it."

"Good," Tolliver said, standing up. "If you'll excuse me, I'll leave you to finish your beer."

Spotted Dog, who had sat where he could see Clint and where Clint could see him, also stood up.

"Oh, one thing, Adams," Tolliver said.

"Yes?"

"Whatever I decide to do," the self-appointed marshal said, "I hope you won't try to get in my way."

Wearily Clint said, "Tolliver, I probably won't even be here. I have no desire to see you in action."

"Good," Tolliver said. "Then it will all work out for the best."

As Tolliver left with Spotted Dog covering his back, Clint wondered just who it would all work out best for.

EIGHTEEN

Almost as Tolliver went out the door, Clint decided to leave Ryland the next morning. He'd done what he could, and Tolliver was right about one thing, it really wasn't his place to interfere. He'd talked to both Roscoe Wells and Dan Tolliver, and neither seemed receptive to what he was telling them. They seemed intent on doing what they wanted to do, no matter what the consequences were. Who was he to try to get them to do differently?

He knew one thing. If Tolliver and his men did shoot down Roscoe Wells and the other three young men, he wasn't going to be around to see it.

Roscoe Wells stared at Ray Carter, Sam Doyle, and Tim Witherspoon. They were all the same age, having grown up together, but even while they were growing up, it was Roscoe Wells who was the leader.

Wells had lied to Clint. He figured since he'd told Clint Adams that they would no longer be at the shack, it was safe to stay there. The other three thought it was a very smart thing to think, something that never would have occurred to them.

So now he stared at them, having told them what Clint Adams had told him. Ray Carter had not, on the other hand, told Sam and Tim what he and Clint had talked about. He just couldn't go against Wells that way.

"What do you think, Roscoe?" Witherspoon asked.

"I think we should show this town that we're more than just a thorn in its side," Wells said. "I say that if we take old Dan Tolliver and shove him up the ass of the town council, this town is ours." His eyes shone, and he was vehement in his belief.

Witherspoon, all caught up in Wells's enthusiasm, said, "Well, I'm with you, Roscoe."

"Me too," Doyle said, because that was what he usually said.

Wells looked at Ray Carter.

"What about you, Ray?"

Carter swallowed and said, "I go along with you all the way, Roscoe, you know that."

"It's settled then," Roscoe Wells said, with great satisfaction. "Let Dan Tolliver come."

Tolliver thought very little of Mark Randall, but the man had thrown this job their way when he and the deputies hadn't had a job for too long. Tolliver didn't know what the problem was. Could it be that his time was coming to an end? That the need for the Dan Tollivers of the world was fading?

No, that couldn't be. As long as there was evil, as long as there were "bad" men, there would be a need for Tolliver and his deputies.

After speaking with Randall, Tolliver was convinced that the Roscoe Wells gang was just such an evil entity that had to be stopped.

Outside the office, Tolliver said to Spotted Dog, "He wants a job with us, doesn't he?"

"I think so," the Indian said, pleased that the older man had been able to see that. In his most lucid moments he was indeed the Dan Tolliver of old.

Tolliver turned and looked back at the door of the sheriff's office, then looked at Spotted Dog and said, "Not a chance."

Clint slept with Lydia Burdette that final night in Ryland, but couldn't quite recapture the passion or excitement he'd felt in her father's storeroom. By the next morning he was more than ready to leave Ryland, Kansas, and never give it another thought.

Clint went to the livery to retrieve Duke, his big black gelding. He was traveling without his rig this time, which was just as well. He wanted to put plenty of distance between himself and this town as soon as possible. His ultimate destination was Labyrinth, Texas, his unofficial base. It was in Labyrinth that he usually rested before heading off again with no particular destination in mind. It seemed these days that the only time he did know where he was going was when he was headed for Labyrinth. He supposed that when the time came for him to settle down it would be there, but he was not ready to think about that yet.

When he rode out of town he passed by the hotel. Instinctively he knew he was being watched, probably from one of the windows. He didn't turn his head, though, and simply continued out of town.

From the window of his room, Spotted Dog watched as Clint Adams rode by. He was very satisfied to see that the man was leaving Ryland. He did not want Tolliver to have to deal with Adams, but he knew one thing. Their paths would cross again someday, and when that time came, Tolliver's Deputies were going to need someone in their number who could match up against the Gunsmith with a gun.

NINETEEN

It was several days later when Clint heard about what had happened in Ryland. He had deliberately avoided reading any newspapers because he didn't want to know what had happened. He was in a saloon in a small town called Haywood, Texas, when he overheard a conversation between two men to his right at the bar.

"Damnedest thing," a man said. "Tolliver and his men just shot down these four, easy as you please."

"No kidding," another man said.

"And then they just rode out."

"What about the sheriff?"

"What could he do?" the first man asked. "The town hired Tolliver to do it. The man was just doing his job. Sheriff can't touch him for that, can he?"

"I guess not."

"Damnedest thing . . ."

"Excuse me," Clint said to the man.

The speaker turned and stared at Clint.

"I couldn't help overhearing. Where did you read about this?"

"Didn't," the man said. "Saw it myself."

"Really?"

"Just a few days ago."

"What day?"

The man told him, and Clint realized that it had happened the afternoon of the same day he left. If it was true, Tolliver had not wasted any time.

"You made good time getting here," Clint said, wondering if the man was telling the truth about seeing the incident.

"Had a job waiting for me here, mister," the man said. "What of it?"

"Nothing," Clint said. "Sorry I interrupted."

Clint left the saloon and walked to the office of the local newspaper.

"Can I help you?" an ink-smudged clerk asked.

"I'd like to know if you have anything on a shooting that took place in Ryland, Kansas, a few days ago?"

"Tolliver and his boys? Sure do."

The clerk handed Clint a copy of the local paper and pointed to the article. It stated that Dan Tolliver and his deputies had once again cleaned up a town by attempting to bring to justice four outlaws who were terrorizing it.

During the attempt the four men had tried to shoot it out with the deputies, and all were killed.

"Thanks," Clint said. He handed the paper back and left the office feeling sick.

His original opinion of Tolliver and his men had been accurate. All that talk by Tolliver about assessing the situation and acting accordingly was just so much bullshit. He'd gone out the very next day and executed those four young men.

For about a half hour Clint wondered if he would have been able to stop the shooting if he'd stayed, but then he realized how foolish that was. Chances were he'd have ended up killing someone, or getting killed himself. He'd stuck his nose in where it didn't belong, had tried his best to head off a showdown, and it hadn't worked. He was going to have to accept that fact.

He knew one thing, though. The next time he crossed paths with Tolliver and his deputies there would be no pretense of civility. He had all the proof he needed now that Dan Tolliver and his men were nothing but bounty hunters—or worse.

They were killers operating under the pretense of upholding the law.

TWENTY

One Year Later . . . New Mexico

Clint had been staying at Sonny Craig's ranch outside of Circle Creek, New Mexico, for several days without being aware that his friend was having some problems. The first inkling he had was when the sheriff of Circle Creek came out to the ranch to talk to Craig. The rancher and Clint were walking the grounds when Craig noticed the rider approaching.

"Know who it is?" Clint asked.

"Looks like the sheriff."

"Is there a problem?"

Craig, a big, potbellied man who was used to taking care of his own problems said, "Nothing I can't handle. I better see what he wants."

As Craig walked over to greet the sheriff, another man came up alongside of Clint. It was

Dave Craig, Sonny's twenty-three-year-old son.
He was taller than his father and well built.
Physically he resembled the elder Craig not at
all, taking after his late mother, instead.

"What's going on, Dave?" Clint asked.

He didn't know Dave Craig that well, and in
fact had not seen Sonny in almost ten years.
The man had been inviting him to his New
Mexico ranch for years, and Clint had finally
been in the vicinity and stopped in to visit.
Sonny made him promise to stay several days,
maybe a week.

"Pop didn't tell you?" Dave Craig asked.

"Tell me what?"

"We're having some trouble with rustlers,"
Dave said. "We've been missing some beef lately."

"What's lately?"

"Past few months, I guess."

"Months? Any idea who's doing it?"

"No," Dave said, "but maybe that's why the
sheriff's here."

Together they watched while Sonny Craig
talked with the sheriff, who was a tall, dark-
haired man Clint hadn't met. He had passed
through Circle Creek on his way to the Craig
ranch without stopping, so there had been no
need.

"What's the sheriff's name?" Clint asked.

"Tate," Dave said, "Ed Tate. Know him?"

Clint shook his head.

"Never heard of him."

"Doesn't have much of a rep, I guess, but he's
been a good man so far."

"How long has he had the job?"

"A few months, I guess."

The conversation went on a little longer, and Sonny seemed to be growing agitated. The sheriff made a placating gesture with his hands, then mounted up and rode away. Sonny stared after him for a few moments, then turned and walked back to where Clint and Dave were standing.

"What's goin' on, Pop?"

Sonny hesitated, looking at Clint.

"I told Clint about the rustling."

"I didn't want to bother you with our trouble," Sonny said to Clint.

"What did the sheriff have to say?" Clint asked. "Did he find out who's been doing the rustling?"

"Come back to the house, Clint," Sonny said. "I'll tell you about it over a drink."

"Should I come too, Pop?"

"No," Sonny said, "you've got work to do. I'll talk to you about it later."

"But—"

"Get back to work, Dave."

"Yes, sir."

"When you see Abel, send him to the house."

Dave firmed his jaw and said, "Yes, sir."

Abel McKane was Sonny's foreman, and apparently Dave didn't like the man. Clint had had more than one inkling of that during his stay. Dave thought that he should be the foreman, but Sonny felt he was still too young and inexperienced.

"Shouldn't you be telling Dave this before me?" Clint asked as they walked back to the house.

"I'll tell him about it later," Sonny said. "Now that you know what's going on, I'd like to bounce a couple of things off you."

"Why didn't you tell me when I got here?"

Sonny waved a hand.

"Like I said, I didn't want to bother you. I thought maybe nothing would happen while you were here."

"And something has?"

"Yes, we lost some more beef last night," Sonny said angrily.

"Do you know who took it?"

Sonny hesitated, then said, "I've had an idea about that for a while, and I was hoping the sheriff would confirm it for me."

"And did he?"

"Let's get that drink."

In the house Sonny took Clint to the den, stopping only to talk to Consuela, the woman who ran his house, about dinner.

In the den he poured two glasses of brandy and handed one to Clint. They both sat on soft divans facing each other.

"This rustling has been goin' on for months," Sonny said. "Nothing big, mind you, just a steer here and there, but even that piles up, you know? When you figure what beef is going for a pound, I'm losing good money even when one animal is taken."

"You said you had an idea who was doing it?" Clint reminded him.

"Yeah," Sonny said. "There are some squatters in the area. They claimed a piece of land, built themselves a little shack, and think they're gonna put down roots."

"What do you mean, they claimed the land?"

"It's a piece that's adjacent to mine, west of here. Nobody owns it, really, and they just arrived one day and started building."

"What's wrong with that?" Clint asked. "If I remember correctly, that's how you started all those years ago."

"Yeah, maybe," Sonny said, "but I didn't steal anybody's beef."

"So you think they're doing it? Not some gang of rustlers, maybe from across the border?"

"I thought that for a while, but there's no indication of that kind of activity going on. For one thing, nobody else has been hit, only me."

"And you think it's them because their land is right near yours?"

"It ain't their land!" Sonny said.

"Well, right now it sounds like it's nobody's."

"I'm tryin' to change that," Sonny said.

"How?"

"I'm trying to file on that land as an extension of my place," Sonny said. "If I get that pushed through, I can throw them off."

"And if not?"

"I'm not gonna let them take any more of my beef without doin' something about it, that's for sure."

"What did you have in mind?" Clint asked. "Taking the law into your own hands?"

"There was a time I would have done that."

"I know."

"This time, though, I'm thinking of hiring someone to do it for me."

"Like who?" Clint asked. Then he added hastily, "If you're thinking of offering me—"

"No, no," Sonny said, "I know better than that, Clint. I know how you feel about hiring out your gun."

"Then who did you have in mind?"

Sonny Craig sat back in his chair, crossed his legs, and asked, "Have you ever heard of Tolliver's Deputies?"

TWENTY-ONE

"You can't be serious," Clint said.

"You've heard of Tolliver, then?"

"Heard of him and met him," Clint said. "You can't seriously be thinking of hiring him."

"Why not?"

"The man's a killer, Sonny," Clint said. "He and his men hire their guns out, and they wear badges to make it appear legal."

"He's got a reputation for getting things done," Sonny said. "That's what I need, Clint. Somebody who can get this thing done."

"What thing?"

"I want to get rid of those rustlers."

"You just finished saying they weren't rustlers," Clint said, "just squatters."

"What's the difference what you call them?" Sonny demanded. "They're stealing my cattle."

82

"Then why don't you go and talk to them?" Clint asked. "Find out why they're stealing your cattle. Maybe they're hungry. Maybe if you offered to sell them some—"

Sonny laughed aloud.

"If they were willing to buy beef, do you think they'd be stealing it?" he demanded.

"But you don't even know for sure that it's them," Clint argued.

"Tolliver can decide that when he gets here."

"Wait a minute," Clint said, sitting forward in his chair. "You've already contacted him?"

"Contacted him and sent him his initial payment," Sonny Craig said. "He'll be here day after tomorrow."

Clint sat back in his chair.

"You're making a big mistake, Sonny."

"It's those squatters that made the mistake, Clint, when they decided to steal from me."

Clint was about to say something else when another man appeared at the door. It was Abel McKane, a big, capable-looking man in his early thirties. He had black hair and a half day beard stubble.

"You wanted to see me, Mr. Craig?"

"That's right, Abel," Craig said. "Have a seat." Clint noticed that he didn't offer the man a glass of brandy. He knew for a fact that McKane had been foreman for the past four years, and had worked for Craig two years prior to that. He had to be pretty impressive at his job to be named foreman that soon, but after six years of employment he still called Craig "Mister."

McKane came into the room, nodded to Clint, and sat down.

"I just talked to Ed Tate, Abel," Craig said. "He still can't find any hard evidence that the squatters have been taking our beef."

"What do we do, then?" McKane asked.

"We'll wait for Tolliver to get here before we do anything else."

McKane tossed Clint a sidelong look.

"Clint knows about Tolliver," Craig said, "and he doesn't approve."

"We could try to take care of the problem ourselves, Mr. Craig."

"No," Craig said, "I think this time I'm happier to have someone take care of it for us, Abel."

"What do you want me to do, sir?"

"I just want you to keep the men in line until Tolliver gets here. When he and his men arrive, he'll take full command of the situation."

"Yes, sir."

"All right, that's all."

"Yes, sir."

McKane got up to leave, but Craig spoke again before he reached the door.

"One more thing, Abel."

"Yes, sir?"

"I'll be telling my son the same thing in a little while," Craig said.

"Yes, sir?"

"I want you to keep a close eye on him for the next few days. I don't want him doing anything stupid."

"Yes, sir," McKane said, "I'll keep an eye on him."

"Good," Craig said, "that's all."

After the man left, Clint asked, "Does his job include playing nursemaid?"

"It includes anything I tell him it includes," Craig said, "and that includes keeping my son out of trouble. Dave has a hair-trigger temper that sometimes gets the better of him. He got that from his mother—that and his looks."

"He's a fine-looking young man, Sonny," Clint said, standing up.

"Clint," Craig said, "I know I'm doing the right thing bringing Tolliver in."

"I'm sorry, Sonny," Clint said, "but I can't agree with you."

"I'm sorry, then."

"So am I," Clint said. "I think I'll take Duke for a run, stretch his legs."

"Sure," Craig said. "Consuela says dinner will be ready at five sharp."

"I'll be here."

"Would you send Dave in if you see him, Clint?" Craig asked.

"Sure."

Clint left the house and walked to the barn to saddle Duke. He was going to poke his nose in where it didn't belong one more time. He didn't believe in coincidence, and the fact that he was once more crossing paths with Tolliver in a bad situation led him to believe that he was being given a second chance to set things right. A year ago four young men had died because he gave up on trying to help.

That wasn't going to happen this time.

TWENTY-TWO

Clint did indeed see Dave Craig on his way to the barn, and relayed his father's message.

"He had to tell you and McKane first, didn't he?" Dave asked. He seemed angry, but more disappointed.

"I don't know what to say to that, Dave."

"Never mind, Clint," Dave said. "You don't have to say anything. I'll take it up with my father."

Clint was thankful for that; he did not want to be put in the position of explaining to Dave that his father thought him immature and inexperienced.

Before he reached the barn, he also ran into Abel McKane, the foreman.

"What do you think of the boss's plan, Adams?" McKane asked.

"I think he's making a mistake, McKane,"

Clint said. "Tolliver's a killer, and while he and his men may have their place, dealing with squatters is not it."

"Have you met Tolliver, seen him in action?" McKane asked.

"I've met him," Clint said, "but thankfully I haven't seen him in action, and I don't want to."

"Does that mean you'll be leaving?"

Clint started to say no, but instead said, "I don't know."

"Well, I've got work to do," McKane said.

"What do you think of your boss's idea, McKane?" Clint asked.

"This is his place, Adams," McKane said, without hesitation. "He makes the rules, and I follow them. That's my job."

"What if you thought he was making a bad move?" Clint asked.

"He hasn't made one yet in all the time I've worked for him," the man said. "I've got to go."

As the foreman walked away, Clint couldn't fault the man for knowing his job. He went to the barn, saddled Duke, and took him out for that run—only it wasn't just to stretch his legs.

He went looking for that piece of land the squatters had settled on.

TWENTY-THREE

The squatters—and that was the way Clint thought of them, for want of another word—were not difficult to find. When he reached the general area where they were supposed to be, he saw smoke, from either a camp fire or a chimney, and followed it straight to them.

Elizabeth Carmondy saw the rider approaching and ran inside to get her father and her brother.

"What is it, girl?" Frank Carmondy asked.

"A rider, Papa."

"Ben," Frank Carmondy said, "get my rifle."

Ben Carmondy, seventeen and already as tall as his six-foot father, retrieved the rifle from its place above the fireplace.

"Stay inside, girl," Carmondy told his daughter, even though he was sure the nineteen-year-old would not heed his word. Ever since her mother died three years ago the girl had become unmanageable.

So all three Carmondys went outside to face the rider, who was now approaching the house.

As Clint approached the house, three people came out the front door and stood on the flimsy excuse for a porch. There were two men and a woman. One man carried a rifle and appeared to be in his late forties or early fifties. The other man and the woman had to be his son and daughter. The man was a boy, really, no more than sixteen or seventeen, though almost fully grown physically. The woman was probably not yet twenty, and was pretty—very pretty.

"Whataya want?" the man demanded, pointing the rifle at Clint as he reined Duke in.

Clint stared back at the man and said, "Well, for starters, I want you to point that rifle someplace else."

"I asked you what you want, mister," the man repeated. "Don't make me ask again."

"My name is Clint Adams," he said, "and if you live here I want to talk to you."

"About what?"

"About helping you."

"We don't need no help," the man said.

"And if we did," the girl chimed in, "we wouldn't need it from no stranger."

"Hush, girl!" the man said.

"Mister," Clint said, "you don't need that rifle. All I want to do is talk."

"Go ahead and talk."

"Not while you're pointing that gun at me."

"That's fine with me," the man said. "Turn around and ride back the way you came, then."

Clint studied the man for a moment and saw that he wasn't about to back down.

"All right, then," Clint said. "I understand you've been having some trouble with one of your neighbors."

"My neighbors?" the man asked, frowning. "What the hell are you talkin' about?"

"I'm talking about Sonny Craig."

"That bastard!" The man raised his rifle to shoulder level. "If you're a friend of his, you better ride, mister."

"He says you're stealing some of his beef."

"And he hired you to come out here and scare us off our land?"

"He didn't hire me to do anything," Clint said, "but he is hiring somebody."

"So what are you doin' here?"

"I'm here to help you, like I said. To warn you, anyway."

"Why?"

Clint didn't answer. Instead he looked around. Other than the little house and a lean-to that seemed to be serving as a barn, there weren't any more buildings around. No other people either.

"Is it just the three of you here?"

The man laughed humorlessly.

"No, my seventeen hands are out ridin' and ropin'," he said. "What's it to you?"

Why was Sonny Craig hiring Tolliver to deal with a man and his two children? Something wasn't right here.

"What's your name?" Clint asked.

"Carmondy," the man answered, "Frank Carmondy."

The name didn't mean anything to Clint. Did it mean anything to Craig? Was Carmondy an old enemy of some sort?

"Mister," Carmondy said, "I ain't gettin' any more comfortable holding this rifle on you. You got more to say, then say it and git!"

"Mr. Carmondy," Clint said, "I don't understand what's happening myself, but apparently Craig thinks you've been stealing some of his cattle."

"We found that steer!" the boy said. "It was already dead!"

"Quiet, boy!"

"But, Pa," the boy said, "he's callin' us thieves. We ain't thieves."

"In the eyes of the law we are," the girl said. "That steer wasn't ours and we ate it."

"We was hungry!" the boy argued.

"One steer?" Clint asked. "One dead steer?"

The man looked away from his children back at Clint.

"That was it," Frank Carmondy said. "We found it, and we was hungry."

"How did Craig find out about it?"

"I don't know," Carmondy said, "but ever since then he's been harassin' us, tryin' to get us off this land, callin' us thieves. He can't prove nothin', though."

"He may not have to," Clint said.

"What's that mean?"

"If you'll let me come inside, Mr. Carmondy," Clint said, "maybe we could talk about it."

The man didn't move, but Clint could see he was thinking.

"If you like," Clint said, "you could take my gun."

That seemed to make up the man's mind.

"Well . . . I guess we could talk. You sure you don't work for Craig?"

"No," Clint said, "I don't work for Craig or anyone else."

"Don't believe him, Pa!" the boy said.

"I told you to hush, Ben," Carmondy said. He lowered the rifle. "All right, mister, come on inside."

TWENTY-FOUR

The inside of the house was simple. The chairs and tables had been built probably right after the house. The house was small, but sturdy, like the furniture. Whoever had built it knew what he was doing.

"Did you do all this yourself?" Clint asked.

"The three of us," Frank Carmondy said.

"Pa did most of it," the girl said.

"I helped," Ben said.

"You both helped," Carmondy said. "Ben, set this rifle back on the wall for me."

"But, Pa—" Ben Carmondy tossed a warning look Clint's way.

"Do as I say, boy."

"Yes, Pa."

"Elizabeth, bring us some coffee."

"Yes, Pa."

Up close the girl was startlingly beautiful,

with the smoothest skin Clint had ever seen. He was beyond the age, however, where he did anything more than simply admire nineteen- and twenty-year-old girls—well, most of them, anyway.

"Sit down, Mr. Adams," Carmondy said. "Adams . . . I know that name, don't I?"

"I suspect you might," Clint said. "Where are you from?"

"Virginia," the man said. "Came out west to make a new home for me and my children— although they ain't really children no more."

"I guess not," Clint said. "How old is Ben? Sixteen?"

"I'm seventeen," Ben said, coming over to sit with the two men.

"Ben," Carmondy said, "me and Mr. Adams was talkin'."

"Aw, Pa," Ben said, "you just said I wasn't a kid no more. Why can't I sit and talk too?"

Carmondy opened his mouth to protest, then closed it as he realized his son was right.

"And me?" Elizabeth asked, bringing over two cups and a pot of coffee.

"Elizabeth," Carmondy said, "this is men talk. You may be growed up and nineteen, but you're still a female."

"Pa—"

"Elizabeth!"

"Yes, Pa."

She moved away from the table to the stove. Clint figured she had given in so easily because

the house was small and she would hear what
was being said anyway.

Carmondy poured out two cups of coffee and
set the pot back down on the table.

"All right, Mr. Adams," he said, "you might
as well talk to me now."

"Mr. Carmondy, have you ever heard of a
man named Tolliver, Dan Tolliver?"

Carmondy thought a moment then said,
"Can't say as I have. Who is he?"

"He's a hired killer, really," Clint said, and
went on to explain about Tolliver and his deputies.

"And that's who Mr. Craig has sent for
because we ate one steer?" Elizabeth asked
anxiously.

"Elizabeth!" Frank Carmondy scolded.

"Pa, that man is sendin' a killer after you!"

"After us," Ben Carmondy said, and everyone in the room looked at him.

"Your boy's right, Mr. Carmondy," Clint said,
after a moment.

"Well, what do you expect me to do about it?"
Carmondy asked.

"Can you fight seven men?" Clint asked.

"Maybe not," Carmondy said, "but I ain't
leavin' this land. The last thing I promised
my wife before she died was that I'd take our
children out here and make a home for them."

"But does it have to be here?" Clint asked.

Carmondy firmed his jaw and said, "This is
where we ended up, and this is where we'll
stay."

"Then you'll probably have to face Tolliver," Clint said. "Or go and talk to Craig before this whole thing gets out of hand."

Carmondy frowned.

"I guess I could do that," he said. "Talk to Craig, I mean, and explain."

"I think that might be a good idea."

Carmondy looked at Clint then.

"What's your interest in this?"

"I'll tell you the truth, Mr. Carmondy," Clint said. "I'm a houseguest of Sonny Craig, but when I heard about this I was against it."

"You say you're friends with Craig?" Carmondy asked.

"Should I get the rifle again, Pa?" Ben asked.

"Hush up," Carmondy said.

"I am friends with him, yes, but like I said, I don't think hiring Tolliver is the right thing to do. I don't hold with hiring killers."

"What's Craig gonna think when he finds out you was out here talkin' to me?"

"Well," Clint said, "I guess I'll either have to move into a hotel, or move on."

"You're riskin' your friendship with him for us?" Elizabeth asked.

Clint looked at her.

"I don't like seeing innocent people persecuted, or worse, Elizabeth," Clint said. "Besides, I don't think the Sonny Craig I used to know would do this. I'd like to find out what's behind it." He looked at Carmondy. "Did you know Craig before you came here?"

"No, never met the man."

"Had a run-in with him before the steer?"

"No," Craig said, "we didn't have no contact until we ate that steer."

"We was starvin' then, Mr. Adams," Ben said. "Since then Elizabeth planted a garden behind the house, and me and Pa, we do odd jobs."

"That's how you live?" Clint asked.

"So far," Carmondy said. "I'm a carpenter by trade. I hope to get some work doin' carpentry."

"If this house and table and chairs are any indication, I don't think you'll have too much trouble finding that kind of work."

"First off, though, I got to clear this up with Craig," Carmondy pointed out.

"I think that's wise."

"Mr. Adams?"

"Yes, Elizabeth?"

"Would you go to talk to Mr. Craig with my pa? Since you know him, I mean?"

"If he wants me to, I will, Elizabeth."

"Pa?" she said.

"I like to solve my own problems, girl," Carmondy said. But then he added, "I guess it wouldn't hurt if he came along, though."

"Might keep you from gettin' shot at," Ben said.

They all looked at Ben again. He seemed to have a knack for getting right to the point.

TWENTY-FIVE

They discussed it and decided that there was no time like the present to talk to Sonny Craig.

"There might still be time to head off Tolliver and his boys if we act now," Clint reasoned.

"I'll saddle my horse."

"Can I come, Pa?" Ben asked.

"We only got one horse, Ben."

"But, Pa, I can run—"

"Stay here with you sister, Ben."

"Pa—"

"Go and saddle the horse, son."

"Yes, Pa."

"I'll put on my boots," Carmondy said, and for the first time Clint realized that the man hadn't been wearing any. Earlier on he'd been too preoccupied looking at the rifle, and then later the man's feet were under the table.

Carmondy left the room, leaving Clint alone with Elizabeth.

"I'm much obliged to you for doin' this, Mr. Adams," she said.

"Call me Clint."

"Clint," she said, blushing. "I ain't never called a growed man by his first name before. Ma always said it was disrespectful."

"Well, you're a grown woman now, aren't you, Elizabeth?"

"Yeah, I reckon—"

"And we're friends now, aren't we?"

"I suppose—"

"Then there's nothing disrespectful about calling a friend by his first name, is there?"

She thought a moment, then shrugged and said, "I guess not."

TWENTY-SIX

The horse Frank Carmondy rode was nothing more than a plow horse, so it took a lot longer to get back to the Craig ranch than it had taken Clint to get there from the ranch. In addition, Carmondy didn't own a saddle, so he had to ride bareback.

As Clint and Carmondy were riding up to the house, several men stopped to watch them, one of which was Dave Craig.

"Hey!" Dave called. "Clint. What are you doin' here with him?"

"He came to talk to your father, Dave."

"Him? He's the one's been stealin' our beef. Don't you know that?"

"We'll talk to your father about it, Dave," Clint said. "Where is he?"

Dave didn't answer. Instead he turned to

talk to the men, more of whom were starting to gather around.

"He's the one's been stealin' our beef!" he yelled. "We just gonna let him ride in here, nice as you please?"

The men began to respond.

"Whataya want us to do, Dave?" one said.

"Yeah," another shouted, "tell us what to do."

"Drag him down off that horse," Dave said. "Teach him what it means to steal somebody else's cattle."

"I better git," Carmondy said. "If I had my rifle I'd—"

"You don't need your rifle," Clint said, "and you don't have to go. Just sit tight."

"Well?" Dave shouted.

"Take it easy, Dave," Clint called out. "You don't want to start any trouble."

"He started the trouble when he stole our cows," Dave said, pointing at Carmondy. "Come on, men, drag him down off that horse."

"Yeah, let's do it!" someone yelled, and suddenly eight or ten men were advancing toward Clint and Carmondy.

"Get back!" Clint shouted. "Dave, call them off."

"You sidin' with him, Clint?" Dave yelled.

"I'm not siding with anyone, Dave," Clint said. "He's here to talk to your father. He's here to . . ."

Nobody was listening. The men were closing

in, and suddenly hands were on Carmondy, pulling him from his horse. Clint knew he had to do something. If the man was hurt, it would be his fault.

As Carmondy struck the ground, Clint drew his gun and fired into the air. It got quiet, and everybody stopped and looked at him.

"I'll shoot the next man who touches him," Clint said.

They all knew who Clint was, knew his reputation, and they believed him. As they backed off, Carmondy got to his feet and began brushing himself off. At the same time the front door of the house opened and Sonny Craig came running out. From another direction came Abel McKane.

"What the hell is goin' on?" McKane demanded, first to reach the scene. He stared up at Clint, who still had his gun out, but before he could say anything, Sonny Craig reached them.

"What the hell?" he bellowed. "McKane, what's goin' on here?"

"I don't know, Mr. Craig," McKane said, "I just got here myself."

"It's Clint, Pa," Dave said. "He brought that cattle thief in here, nice as you please, and then he took a shot at us."

Craig looked up at Clint and saw that he was still holding his gun.

"You ass," he said to his son. "If Clint Adams took a shot at you, somebody'd be dead right now."

"But, Pa—"

"Shut up!" Craig looked up at Clint. "What's goin' on, Clint?"

"I fired in the air, Sonny," Clint explained, "to keep anything ugly from happening."

"Nothin' ugly would have happened, Clint, if you hadn't brought that man here," Craig said. "What the hell were you thinkin'?"

"I was thinking that you two could talk and iron out your differences, Sonny," Clint said. "Do you really want to talk about this out here?"

"No," Craig said, "I don't want to talk about it at all." He looked at Carmondy and said, "Get back on your horse and get off my property."

Carmondy looked up at Clint and said, "I told you this wouldn't work."

He climbed back up onto his horse, turned, and rode away.

"Sonny, you're being bullheaded," Clint said. "Can we go inside and talk?"

"About what?" Craig asked. "About why you brought that man to my home? I think you've made your feelin's real clear, Clint. I think it would be best if you cleared out. You're not welcome in my house anymore."

"Sonny," Clint called, as the man turned and walked away, "there's no reason to hire Tolliver for—"

But Craig wasn't listening. He just kept walking toward the house.

"Better get your stuff, Adams, and clear out

like the man said," McKane told him. "Your horse will be waitin' when you come back out."

Clint holstered his gun, stepped down, and followed Sonny Craig to the house.

TWENTY-SEVEN

"Sonny!" Clint shouted as he entered the house.

Sonny Craig turned and pointed a finger at Clint.

"Don't be yellin' at me in my own house, Clint Adams!" he bellowed.

"Sonny, you're makin' a big mistake here," Clint said, trying once again to reason with the man.

"My big mistake was invitin' you here, thinkin' you were the same man I knew."

"I haven't changed, Sonny," Clint said, "it's you who have changed."

"Why? Because I won't abide havin' another man steal my beef?"

"No, because there was a time you'd handle it yourself and not call in hired gunmen."

Craig pointed again and said, "Those days

are gone. I do things within the law now."

Clint couldn't believe what he was hearing.

"Hiring Dan Tolliver is doing things within the law?" he asked.

"Well, I'm not takin' the law into my own hands, am I?" Craig demanded.

"By hiring Tolliver that's exactly what you're doing," Clint reasoned.

"Ah," Craig said, waving his hand, "that doesn't make any sense. I ain't liftin' a hand against those people."

Clint couldn't believe that Craig didn't see that hiring someone else to do it was like doing it himself. Talking to the man was like talking to a barn wall.

"Clint," Craig said, "I meant what I said out there. If you aren't sidin' with me, then you're against me."

"I can't side with you on this, Sonny," Clint said. "You're sending seven gunmen to kill a man and his two children."

"Bah!" Craig said. "He's got help, you just haven't seen them. Why did you ride over there anyway, Clint?"

"I wanted to see what they were like."

"Well, you saw what they wanted you to see, and nothin' more."

"Sonny—"

"I don't want to talk anymore, Clint," Craig said. "No more."

The man turned and walked away and disappeared down a hall. Clint stared after him

for a few moments, then went upstairs to collect his belongings.

When he came out he was surprised to find
the foreman himself, Abel McKane, holding his
horse for him. The rest of the men had dis-
banded and gone back to work.

"Thanks, McKane," Clint said, taking Duke's
reins from the man.

"Sorry this had to happen, Adams."

"Yeah, me too," Clint said, mounting up. He
looked down at the man and said, "He's wrong,
McKane. You know he's wrong."

"He's my boss, Adams."

"Just because he pays you doesn't mean you
have to think like him."

"I have to be loyal."

"Loyalty will only take you so far, McKane,"
Clint said. "At some point you've got to start
using your own common sense."

TWENTY-EIGHT

Clint wanted to go back and talk to the Carmondys. He could imagine what they must be thinking, and that bothered him. What also bothered him was the fact that he was getting involved in other people's problems again, but he couldn't help it. There was no way the Carmondys could stand up to Tolliver and his deputies, no way in hell. He had to do something.

He decided to ride to town and get himself a hotel room first, then walk over and see the sheriff, Ed Tate. Maybe the sheriff was the kind of man who would listen to reason.

He hoped.

"What happened?" Elizabeth Carmondy asked as her father dismounted.

"Put the horse up, Ben."

"But, Pa—"

"Do as I say, boy," Frank Carmondy said.

"Yes, Pa."

As Ben led the plow horse away, Elizabeth said, "Tell me what happened."

"Clint Adams was wrong," Carmondy said. "Craig didn't want to talk at all. He's got it into his head that we're stealin' his cattle, and that's all there is to it."

"What are we gonna do, Pa?"

Carmondy looked at his daughter, who was the spitting image of her beautiful mother. When he was talking to her it was almost as if Frank Carmondy was talking to his beloved wife.

"We're gonna stay here, Elizabeth," he said. It was all he could do not to call her Beth, as he used to call her mother. Elizabeth was named for her mother, but was never called Beth.

"But, Pa, what about that man and his deputies?" she asked.

"When he gets here and sees it's only us, darlin'," Carmondy said, "what's he gonna do, kill us?"

Frank Carmondy went into the house, leaving Elizabeth standing there with his words ringing in her ears.

TWENTY-NINE

Clint had ridden through Circle Creek on his way to Sonny Craig's ranch. It was not a large town, but it was a prosperous one. It had almost two of everything it needed: hotel, saloon, whorehouse. What kept it from being a large town was that it had only one of everything else.

He rode past the sheriff's office, debated stopping in right away, then decided to wait. First he'd put Duke up in the livery, then check into the hotel. After that a meal would go down very nicely. Once all that was done he'd be ready to talk to the town lawman.

Too often of late Clint had been running into town sheriffs who, years ago, never would have been able to hold the job. There was a time when a town sheriff had to have certain attributes for the job. He had to be

111

smart, fair, and trustworthy. Now none of the three seemed to apply. In some towns you had to know somebody, and in some towns the only requirement was a willingness to pin on the badge—and a lot of men only had that because they thought they could get something for nothing out of the job. Maybe a free meal, maybe some items from the General Store—or even something from the local whorehouse.

Clint checked into the hotel and wondered what Sheriff Ed Tate would be like.

Ed Tate looked up from his desk as his deputy, Kal Sawyer, came into the office.

"That friend of Mr. Craig's?"

"Adams?" Tate asked.

Sawyer nodded.

"He's in town."

"Where?"

"Over to the hotel."

"Gettin' a room?"

"It looked like it. Want I should go over and talk to him?"

Sawyer was young, in his mid-twenties, and as overeager as they come. If Tate had only had another choice, he wouldn't have pinned a badge on this boy's chest.

"No, I don't want you to go over there."

"You gonna do it yourself?"

"No."

The deputy frowned.

"Then what are you gonna do, Sheriff?"

"Nothin'."

"Huh?"

"I'm gonna sit here and wait for Clint Adams to come to me."

"Why's he gonna do that?" Sawyer asked.

"Because he's a stranger in my town, with a rep, and if he knows what's good for him, he'll come and see me."

Sawyer looked disappointed and put his hands on his hips.

"Well, how long you gonna wait?"

"It won't be long," Tate said. "It won't be long at all."

"Sheriff—"

"Go make some rounds, boy."

"I made my rounds. That's when I saw—"

"Then go and get somethin' to eat, Kal! Just get outta here!"

"Well, sure, Sheriff," Sawyer said, "you ain't got to tell me but once."

As the deputy left, Tate sat back in his chair. He'd seen Adams out at the Craig ranch earlier that day. What was the man doing here, checking into the hotel when he was supposed to be a houseguest of Sonny Craig's?

That was what Craig had called him, a "houseguest." Ed Tate had never heard the phrase before, but then he had never owned a house or had guests in it.

Unless he considered the whole town of Circle Creek his house. If that was the case, then Clint Adams was now his houseguest, wasn't he?

• • •

When Clint entered the small restaurant for lunch, he saw the deputy sitting alone at a table. When the deputy looked up and widened his eyes, Clint knew that the young man had recognized him.

Clint sat and ordered steak and vegetables from the waiter, and a pot of coffee. The young deputy was trying to continue to eat his lunch, but it was hard for him to find his mouth because he was keeping his eyes on Clint. It was an off time of day, somewhere between lunch and dinner, so Clint and the deputy were the only two in the place.

"Are you going to keep staring at me the whole time like that, Deputy?" Clint asked.

"What?"

"Because if you are, you might as well come over here and eat with me," Clint said, "that way we can get properly acquainted."

The deputy was at a loss for words for a moment, and then he stammered, "You're in-invitin' me to come over and—and eat with you?"

"That's right," Clint said. "I hate to eat alone, don't you?"

Actually, Clint enjoyed eating alone, but this was an opportunity to find something out about the sheriff before he went to talk to him.

"Come on, son," Clint said, "I'll even pay."

THIRTY

After lunch and an interesting conversation with Deputy Kal Sawyer, Clint crossed the street to the sheriff's office, knocked, and entered.

"Sheriff Tate?"

The man seated at the desk was the same man he'd seen out at Craig's ranch earlier that day.

"That's right."

"My name is Clint Adams."

"I know," Tate said. "I saw you out at Craig's ranch this morning."

Clint approached the desk. Tate stood up, and the two men shook hands. Clint had not gotten a close look at the man before, taking in only that he was tall and dark. Now he could see that the sheriff had a pockmarked face and a scar over his left eye that caused the eyelid to droop a bit. It gave him a menacing look. He appeared to be somewhere in his late thirties.

"What are you doing checking into the hotel?" Tate asked. "I thought you were Sonny Craig's houseguest?"

"I was," Clint said, "but we had a difference of opinion that made it necessary for me to move out."

"A difference of opinion?" Tate asked. "About what?"

"Dan Tolliver."

"Have a seat, Mr. Adams," Tate said, seating himself behind his desk again. "Let's talk."

Clint sat and waited for the sheriff to start.

"I'm no more in favor of Craig hiring Dan Tolliver and his men than you are, Adams."

"I'm glad to hear that, Sheriff."

"But I can't stop him from doing it."

"I'm not so glad to hear that."

"He's within his rights to hire anyone he wants to work for him," Tate said.

"What about when the man he's hiring has a reputation as a killer?"

Tate spread his hands and asked, "What about your own reputation, Mr. Adams? Deserved or not, it's there, isn't it?"

"All right," Clint said, "what you say is true, but I've met Tolliver. I know what he and his men are like. Do you?"

"I've never met any of them—that I know of."

"And have you talked to the Carmondys at all?" Clint asked. "The people Sonny Craig has accused of stealing his cattle?"

"I have," Tate said. "I questioned them as soon as Craig gave me their names."

"Did they tell you they butchered one dead steer that they found?"

"They did."

"And that they ate it to survive?"

"They told me that too."

"And?"

"If they took one, they could have taken more."

"How many more?" Clint asked. "How many more have been stolen?"

"So far? According to Mr. Craig, he's missin' two dozen beefs."

"Two dozen?" Clint said. "You think Carmondy, his son, and his daughter stole twenty-four beefs?"

"I don't think anything," Tate said. "I know they took one."

"One that was already dead."

"That don't make it legal, does it?"

"No, it doesn't," Clint admitted, "but it isn't something they should die for, either."

"Well . . . who says they're gonna die?"

"Come on, Sheriff," Clint said. "Once Tolliver gets here, they're through."

"Have you talked to them?" Tate asked.

"I have."

"Then talk to them again," Tate said. "Bring them a message."

"What message?"

"Tell them to give themselves up to me, and I'll see that they get a fair trial."

"In this county?"

"Wherever," Tate said. "At least they'll be alive. I can keep them away from Tolliver."

Clint stopped for a moment and thought. Once they were in jail Tolliver couldn't get to the Carmondys, and what judge or jury would convict them for stealing one dead steer?

"All right," Clint said, "I'll talk to them."

"Good," Tate said. "See, I don't want anybody gettin' killed any more than you do, Mr. Adams."

"I'm glad to hear that, Sheriff," Clint said, standing up. "You know what?"

"What?"

"This might go over better if you came with me."

"You think so?"

"It couldn't hurt," Clint said, "could it?"

"No," Sheriff Ed Tate said, standing up, "I guess it couldn't."

THIRTY-ONE

It was too late to ride out and talk to the Carmondys that evening, so Clint and Ed Tate agreed to meet early the next morning.

"I appreciate you agreeing to do this with me, Sheriff," Clint said.

"I'm still not sure what your interest in all this is, Adams," Tate said.

"About a year ago I had a chance, I think, to keep Tolliver and his men from killing some people, young men who were no outlaws."

"And you didn't take it?"

"I did some talking, but when it came right down to it, I rode out of town."

"I don't think you could have stopped Tolliver and his men," Tate said. "Not you alone against them."

"Maybe not," Clint said, "but I could have tried to do something."

"So this is your second chance, huh?"

"I guess it is, Sheriff," Clint said. "I'll see you in the morning."

"Early," Tate said, "very early."

"Right."

After Clint Adams left his office, Ed Tate sat back in his chair. Moments later Deputy Kal Sawyer came hurrying in.

"You met him?" Sawyer asked.

"I met him, Kal."

"Jesus, he's impressive, ain't he?"

"Do you think so, Kal?"

"Well, yeah, don't you?"

"Yes, as a matter of fact I do, but then I spoke with him."

"Well, so did I," Sawyer said, proudly.

Tate sat forward in his chair.

"Is that a fact?"

"Well . . . yeah."

"When did you talk to him, Deputy?"

"At lunch," Sawyer said.

"Did I tell you to take him to lunch?"

"Hell, Sheriff, I didn't take him to lunch," Sawyer said. "He took me."

"What?"

"He came in while I was eatin' and invited me to eat with him," Sawyer said, excitedly. "Imagine me eatin' lunch with the Gunsmith?"

"Yeah," Tate said, "yeah, I'm imaginin'. What did the two of you talk about?"

"Well, you, mostly."

"Me?"

"He wanted to know all about you," Sawyer said, "what kind of man you was, and what kind of lawman you was."

"And speaking from your experience with lawmen, you told him, right?"

Suddenly, Sawyer realized that he wasn't just havin' a casual conversation with the sheriff. Tate was annoyed.

"Did I do somethin' wrong, Sheriff?"

Tate rubbed his right hand over his face and waved at the young man with his left.

"No, you didn't do anything wrong, Kal," he said. "Just go and make your rounds, huh?"

"Uh, sure, Sheriff."

"And Kal . . ."

"Yeah?"

"If you talk to Adams again . . ."

"Yeah, Sheriff?"

Tate stared at the young man for a few moments, then said, "Never mind. Just never mind, Kal."

"Uh, sure, Sheriff," Kal Sawyer said, confused, "sure."

Kal had been his deputy for all of three months, ever since his first deputy, George Kent, was killed trying to break up a barroom fight. Kent was another enthusiastic sort. Rather than let the fight sort itself out, he had to step in front of a knife.

Now Kal Sawyer was having lunch with the Gunsmith. How long would it take the young man to spread that story all around town?

Not long, that was for sure.

• • •

Clint left the sheriff's office, crossed the street, and entered the first saloon he came to, the Dixie Saloon. It was half full, and in a short time would be more than half full. Maybe then he could find a poker game to pass the time. Right now all he wanted was a beer and a table to himself.

"Beer," he told the bartender.

He turned with his mug in hand to survey the room. There were plenty of empty tables, but he was hoping for one in a corner. He spotted one and crossed the room to it, but a moment after he sat down he was joined—by a lady.

"Need some company?" she asked.

He looked up and saw a willowy blonde in her late thirties. She had large breasts for a woman of her height and slenderness; lots of pale flesh was practically spilling out the front of her dress.

"For how long?" he asked.

"As long as you want, Mister," she said. "That's my job."

He felt his penis thickening at the sight of her cleavage, but he never paid for female company.

"Maybe later," he told her, "when you're not working."

THIRTY-TWO

Clint woke early the next morning and looked at the woman lying in bed next to him. It had taken him only a few hours of conversation to convince the willowy blonde with the big breasts that she should come back to his room with him after work, no charge.

"You'd have to be real good for it to be no charge," she told him.

He smiled at her confidently and said, "I don't think there will be a problem there."

Later, she agreed.

Clint knew he was a rare man. He enjoyed giving women pleasure. He knew many men who thought that it was a woman's place on earth to give a man pleasure, but he believed there was two ways to experience pleasure— by giving it and receiving it.

The girl's name was Melody Anders, and halfway through the night she agreed.

"No charge," she had said sleepily. "Now just let me sleep a little, will you? I can't keep up with you."

Now he stared down at her as she lay on her back, her big breasts firm and spreading just a little onto her rib cage. He leaned over and teased one of her nipples with his tongue, and then the other. Melody started to squirm, but then her hands came up and took hold of his hair.

"Jesus, you do that good," she said.

"Thanks."

"How come?"

"Lots of practice."

"You've been with a lot of women, haven't you?" she asked.

"Not tonight and this morning," he said, running his tongue between her breasts. "Now it's only you."

"Mmmm," she moaned as he slid a hand between her breasts. "You're gonna leave me too weak to walk."

"You can handle it," he assured her. "You're young."

"Growing older by the minute," she said dreamily as his tongue moved down over her ribs to her navel.

As his tongue moved through the tangle of hair between her legs, he reached up and cupped her breasts, squeezing them tightly.

She moaned, then shuddered as his tongue
entered her. . . .

He got dressed while she watched from the
bed.

"Why do you have to leave so early?" she
asked.

"I have a meeting with the sheriff," he said.
"Besides, you need your sleep."

"That's right," she said, "I didn't get much
last night, did I?"

"It's your own fault for being so lovely," he
said, leaning over to kiss her.

She took hold of his bottom lip with her
teeth so he couldn't pull away immediately,
then released him.

"You're a sweet talker, Clint Adams," she
said. "That makes you a dangerous man."

"I'll see you later," he said, heading for the
door.

"Don't make any promises, Clint," she said
warningly. "You're a sweet talker and a dangerous man, remember?"

Clint met the sheriff in front of his office.
The man looked refreshed and well rested.

"Ready?" Tate asked.

"Sure."

"You look like you didn't get much sleep last
night," Tate said.

"I didn't," Clint said, but didn't offer a
reason.

The sheriff mounted his horse, a good-
looking dappled gray.

"Who's going to do the talking?" the sheriff asked.

"If you don't mind, I thought I would. You can just back up what I say."

"I don't mind," Tate said. "I think they'd listen to you more than they'd listen to me, anyway."

"Maybe," Clint said, as they started out, "but after what happened yesterday, I'm not so sure."

THIRTY-THREE

Just minutes after Clint Adams and Sheriff Ed Tate rode out of town in one direction, self-styled Marshal Dan Tolliver and his deputies rode into town from the other.

Tolliver rode up front, but where he used to ride alone Spotted Dog now rode right alongside of him. Further back Frank Beckett, Carl Rhodes, and the others rode, and as had been the case over the past few months, they were grumbling amongst themselves.

"I still don't get it," Carl Rhodes said. "You been the first deputy for a year, Frank, and it's the Indian who gets to ride with the marshal, it's Spotted Dog who talks for the marshal."

Beckett shrugged.

"Spotted Dog has been with the marshal the

longest, Carl," he said. "We all know that if Dog would take the job the marshal would make him first deputy."

"So what? You're still the first deputy, it don't matter why."

Behind them Harry Chaplin, Gar Haywood, and Les Saxon were listening.

"If the marshal was in his right mind maybe that'd be true," Beckett said.

"That's another thing," Rhodes said. "We all know the marshal ain't been right for months." It was actually longer than that, but it was only in the past few months that Spotted Dog had been unable to keep it hidden from the men. "Why do we still ride with him?"

"We only get hired because of his name, that's why," Chaplin said. "Without him, we'd just be plain old bounty hunters."

"Well, I'll keep ridin' with him," Haywood said, "as long as I don't have to throw any more fights."

Every so often Tolliver would decide to show that he was still boss by fighting Haywood. Haywood, though the largest and strongest of the six men who rode with Tolliver, did not relish going up against Spotted Dog, and it was the Dog who made him let Tolliver win their fights.

"I still don't like the idea of working for a man who ain't right in the head," Les Saxon said.

Rhodes turned in his saddle and said, "You tell Spotted Dog that, Saxon. Go ahead."

Saxon scowled at Rhodes and then looked away. None of them had the guts to stand up to the Indian.

Spotted Dog could hear the grumblings of the men behind him. He knew it was getting harder and harder to keep them together. They'd only stay as long as the money was coming in, and the money would only come in as long as Dan Tolliver lasted.

The money was secondary to Spotted Dog, though. He was still fighting to keep the public from knowing that Dan Tolliver's lucid moments were now very few and far between.

When they rode up in front of the hotel, Tolliver dismounted. Whatever his frame of mind, physically he was sound. He was still able to mount, dismount, and ride, and he could still shoot—if someone told him what to shoot at.

Spotted Dog dismounted, turned, and said, "Saxon, you and Chaplin take the horses to the livery—all but mine and Beckett's."

"Right."

"Frank," Spotted Dog said, "go in with Rhodes and get the rooms."

Spotted Dog would not even allow Tolliver to speak to hotel clerks anymore. He and the marshal usually waited outside for the room keys, and then Spotted Dog would walk Tolliver up to his room and put him to bed.

As far as talking to the people who hired

them, Spotted Dog and Frank Beckett would do that, with Beckett doing the talking as first deputy. That's what they'd be doing this afternoon, riding out to the Craig ranch to talk to Sonny Craig while Tolliver rested in his room. The other men would be charged with making sure that Tolliver didn't talk to anyone, or wander off.

"Here are the keys, Dog," Frank Beckett said, reappearing. He handed Spotted Dog two hotel room keys, one for him and one for Tolliver.

"All right," Spotted Dog said. "I'll take care of the marshal and meet you here in half an hour. Then we'll go out and talk to Craig."

"Right."

Beckett watched Spotted Dog lead a vacant-eyed Tolliver into the hotel lobby and shook his head. How much longer, he wondered, could this go on?

Spotted Dog walked Tolliver to his room, sat him down on the bed, and removed his boots. Suddenly, Tolliver's eyes shifted and he looked at Spotted Dog—really looked at him.

"What's goin' on?"

"You're resting."

"Again?" Tolliver said. "Seems like that's all I do these days."

"We got business in town, Marshal," Spotted Dog said. "You need to rest."

Spotted Dog laid Tolliver down on the bed so that the marshal was lying on his back.

"What would I do without you, Dog?" Tolliver asked.

Spotted Dog looked down at the man he felt such loyalty to and said, "Probably die."

But Tolliver didn't hear him.

THIRTY-FOUR

As Clint and Ed Tate rode up to the Carmondy place, Clint thought that he wouldn't blame them if they didn't want to talk to him after what had happened yesterday at the Craig ranch. Frank Carmondy could have gotten really hurt, and it would have been his fault. He had read Sonny Craig all wrong, and Carmondy could have ended up paying for it.

They had just reined in their horses when Elizabeth Carmondy came around the house. She had probably been out back tending that little garden Ben had mentioned.

"Elizabeth," Clint called.

She squinted at them and said, "Mr. Adams? Who's that with you?"

"It's Sheriff Tate, Elizabeth, from Circle Creek."

"Oh," she said. "Have you come to arrest us?"

132

"No—" Tate started, but she cut him off.

"To arrest my father, then?"

"No, Miss Carmondy," Tate said, "I haven't come to arrest anyone."

"Why are you here, then?"

"Elizabeth," Clint said, "I'd like to talk to your father. Is he around?"

"No," she said. "He and Ben went hunting." She raised her chin defiantly and added, "We need meat."

Clint looked at Tate, who raised his eyebrows.

"What did you want to talk to him about, Mr. Adams?" she asked.

"I don't know that I should discuss that with you, Elizabeth."

"I know what happened at the Craig ranch yesterday," she said, "and I know about that man, Tolliver, coming to town. Is there something else happening that I don't know about?"

"No, not really."

"Then I think you should talk to me, Mr. Adams," she said. "Come inside and I'll make you some coffee—both of you, Sheriff."

"Thank you, ma'am."

They dismounted, tied off their horses, and followed her into the house.

THIRTY-FIVE

Inside they sat at the handmade kitchen table, and Elizabeth brought them coffee. She sat down opposite them without pouring any for herself.

"You're not having any?" Tate asked.

"I don't like coffee, Sheriff Tate," she said. "Now then, which one of you is going to talk?"

"I am," Clint said. "Elizabeth, I think there's only one way to keep your father—and you and your brother—from having to deal with Dan Tolliver and his men."

"And what is that, Mr. Adams?"

"Well—" he started, but then stopped. "Elizabeth, I thought we said you were going to call me Clint. Remember that?"

She ducked her head and then looked back at him.

"Yes, I remember . . . Clint."

"Good."

"Now what's this solution you came up with?"

"I think you should turn yourselves in."

She frowned.

"For what?"

"For stealing cattle—I mean, that one steer."

"That dead one?" she asked, looking amazed. "Who would convict us of that?"

"That's the point," Clint said. "The sheriff will put you in jail for a few days, a judge will hear your case and probably dismiss the charges. After that Tolliver won't be able to touch you."

"Do you really think so?"

Actually, Clint wasn't sure. Tolliver just might go after them anyway—especially if he wasn't in his right mind. Considering the condition he was in mentally a year ago, he was bound to be worse now.

"I'll be honest with you, Elizabeth," he said, "I don't know."

"Well, I don't think it's a good idea."

"Why not?" Sheriff Tate asked.

She switched her eyes to him, after not having looked at him hardly at all.

"Because while we were in jail, Mr. Craig would probably come and take this place over," she said. "When we got out, we'd never be able to get it back, even if that Tolliver man wasn't around."

She had a good point, Clint thought, and he saw that the sheriff thought so too. He saw something else on the sheriff's face—admiration. He wondered if the man was admiring her logic, or if he was smitten with her.

"I don't think my father will agree to it either," she added.

"Well, maybe we should let him hear it and decide for himself," Clint said.

At that moment they heard footsteps on the porch outside. Then the door opened, and both Ben and Frank Carmondy stomped in.

"Adams," Frank Carmondy said. "You come to take me someplace else for me to get beat up?"

"I'm sorry about that, Mr. Carmondy," Clint said, standing up.

"What's the law doin' here?" Carmondy asked Tate. "Craig send you here to arrest me for trespassing yesterday, Sheriff?"

"I'm not here to arrest anyone, Mr. Carmondy," Tate assured him.

"Then what are you doin' here?" he asked. "Both of you." He turned to Ben and said, "Put the rifle away, boy."

Ben looked reluctant to do so, but he walked to the fireplace and replaced it on the wall pegs.

"Well?" Carmondy asked.

"Pa, they came with a suggestion for us," Elizabeth said.

"Oh? What suggestion is that?"

Clint explained to Carmondy what they had in mind.

"Forget it!" Carmondy said when Clint was

finished. "We'd lose this place in a minute if we went to jail."

"But you wouldn't have to face Tolliver," Clint said.

"Ah, let him come. What's he gonna do to us? Is he a real marshal, Sheriff?"

"No, he's not."

"Then he ain't got no legal power, right?"

"That's right."

"So if he kills me, you could arrest him?"

"I sure could."

"See?" Carmondy said.

"What good would that do you, Mr. Carmondy?" Clint asked. "You'd be dead. How would that benefit your children?"

"Maybe," Ed Tate said, "they'd even be dead too. So Dan Tolliver would be in jail, and you three would all be dead."

"And then Craig would come in and take the land anyway," Clint finished.

Carmondy considered what they'd said for a few moments, then said helplessly, "There's got to be another way."

"I can't see one," Clint said.

"Then I'll just have to think of one," Carmondy said. "Now if you fellas will excuse us, we got to prepare dinner."

"Catch something, did you?" Clint asked.

"Yes," Carmondy said, "and it ain't a steer!"

THIRTY-SIX

"Why ain't Marshal Tolliver here himself?" Sonny Craig asked again.

"I explained that before, Mr. Craig," Frank Beckett said. "It was a long ride, and the marshal needed to rest. He wanted to make contact with you without delay, though, so he sent me."

"And you're his first deputy?"

"That's right."

"You're a little young for the job, ain't you?" Craig asked.

"Maybe, but I've been first deputy for a year and it hasn't hurt me yet," Beckett said just the way Spotted Dog had rehearsed him.

"And what about the Indian?" Craig asked. As soon as they had entered the house, it was clear that Craig was uncomfortable with having an Indian there.

138

"This is Spotted Dog," Beckett said. "He's been with Marshal Tolliver longer than anyone."

"What's his job?"

"He's our tracker."

"Well," Craig said, beaming from behind the desk in his den, "you won't be needing him, then."

"Why not?"

"Because I can tell you exactly where the cattle thieves are."

"That's good," Beckett said. He was improvising. They hadn't rehearsed this part. "Why don't you tell me all you know about these thieves? How many are there?"

"Three that we know of, but there's got to be more of 'em." The speaker this time was Dave Craig.

"Why is that?" Spotted Dog asked. Beckett had hesitated, and the moment was going on too long, so Spotted Dog stepped in.

"The number of beefs that's been taken," Sonny Craig said, throwing his son a hard look. Dave had instructions not to speak at all. "It would indicate that there were more than three."

"Well then, those three could probably tell us where the others are," Beckett said, getting back into the play.

"That's right."

"All right, then," Beckett said, "before we start there's the matter of the payment. Half in advance."

Craig stared at the two men, then shook his head.

"I don't know," he said. "I think I'd rather pay the money directly to Marshal Tolliver."

"Mr. Craig," Beckett said, "I'm first deputy. When you're talkin' to me, you're talkin' to Marshal Tolliver. When you put money in my hand, you put money in his hand. Understand?"

That was just the way Spotted Dog had told him to say it.

"I don't know . . ."

"Fine," Beckett said, "I'll go back and tell the marshal the deal is off, you don't want to pay."

"Hey, wait," Craig said, "I want to pay, I just—"

"Half to me now," Beckett said, "the other half to the marshal when the job is done."

"All right," Craig said, "that's all I wanted. I want a chance to meet the marshal himself."

"You'll meet him, Mr. Craig," Beckett said, "I guarantee it."

A bald-faced lie—just the way Spotted Dog told him to say it.

Outside Spotted Dog and Beckett mounted up and rode away from the ranch.

"I thought he wasn't gonna pay," Beckett said.

"You did fine, Frank," Spotted Dog said. "The marshal would have been proud."

Yeah, Beckett thought, if he even knew what was going on.

"What do we do now?" Beckett asked.

"The same thing we always do," Spotted Dog said, "what we're paid to do."

"Dog," Beckett said, "how much longer can this go on?"

"What do you mean?"

"I mean Tolliver gets worse every day," Beckett said. "The men all know it. What happens when he can't even sit a horse?"

Spotted Dog was silent for a moment, staring straight ahead.

"That's not for you, or the others, to worry about," he said finally. "You all get paid."

"Sure, we get paid," Beckett said, "but—"

"That's enough," Spotted Dog said. "That's enough questions, Frank. No more. Just do your job."

Beckett thought about pursuing the subject, then decided against it. His heart was hammering just talking about it this long. He'd been afraid that when he asked the first question, Spotted Dog might kill him on the spot. The longer the conversation went on, the braver he got, and then the more scared.

"Okay, Dog," he said, "whatever you say."

THIRTY-SEVEN

Clint and Sheriff Tate were silent during the ride back to town. Neither said a word until they were back in front of the sheriff's office.

"I still think it was a good idea," Tate said.

"They were right, from their point of view," Clint said. "If they went along with it, they'd lose their land anyway."

"What else can they do?"

Clint scratched his chin and said, "Maybe it's not what else they can do, but what else I can do."

"Like what?"

"Well, if they're telling the truth and they only took that one dead steer, what does that mean?"

"That somebody else stole all the others," Tate reasoned.

"Right. So all I have to do is find out who that somebody else is."

"How do you propose to do that?"

"I don't suppose you'd like to help me."

"I'm a town sheriff, Adams," Tate said, "not a range detective. I can chase rustlers once I see them, but finding them first is not what I'm good at."

"I guess I'll have to look for them myself, then," Clint said.

"You do that," Tate said, "and when you find them, then you call me."

"I'll do that," Clint said. "You taking your horse to the livery?"

"Not yet," Tate said, "but you go ahead."

Clint started away, then turned back.

"Listen, thanks for going out there with me. You didn't have to do that."

Tate shrugged.

"It didn't cost me anything, did it?"

"No."

"Then no problem. Good luck."

"Thanks."

The sheriff went into his office, and Clint started walking Duke back to the livery. On the way he saw Deputy Kal Sawyer running his way, obviously in a hurry to get to the sheriff's office.

"Hey, whoa, Kal!" Clint called out.

"Oh, hi, Mr. Adams," Sawyer said. "I can't stop and talk now. I got to find the sheriff."

"He just went into his office, Kal," Clint said.

"He did? Thanks."

"What's the big rush?"

"I got to tell him," Sawyer said breathlessly, "that Marshal Tolliver and his deputies are in town."

"When did they get here?" Clint asked, frowning.

"This mornin'," Sawyer said. "I got to go, Mr. Adams."

"Okay, then," Clint said, "go ahead."

Clint turned and watched the young deputy run toward the sheriff's office, then thought of something.

"Where are they staying?" he called out.

"At the hotel," Sawyer called back, and kept running.

Big help, Clint thought. There were two hotels in town.

He had another option now. Tolliver was in town. Before he started looking for rustlers, he could go over to the hotel and talk to him. He hadn't been very receptive a year ago, in Ryland, though, so what was going to make him more receptive now? Especially if his mind had slipped further?

Clint decided to take care of Duke, then get some food in his belly before making his final decision about his next move. In fact, maybe his next move wouldn't even be till tomorrow.

What could happen today? After all, Tolliver and his men had just arrived.

Harry Chaplin and Les Saxon were coming out of the Dixie Saloon when Chaplin grabbed

Saxon's arm and pointed across the street.

"Who's that?"

"Who?" Saxon asked.

"That man walkin' that big black horse."

"Where?" Saxon asked. He'd had more to drink than Chaplin had. They were supposed to go back to the hotel and relieve Gar Haywood, who was on watch with the marshal. They'd take over, and Haywood would go for a drink.

"Right there," Chaplin said. "Jesus, that's Clint Adams."

"Adams?" Saxon said, squinting. "What's he doin' here?"

"I don't know," Chaplin said. "Where was that we saw him last?"

"Kansas, wasn't it?"

"Was it?" Chaplin asked, rubbing his jaw. "Yeah, that's right, a year ago. Ryland, Kansas."

"And now he's here?" Saxon asked. "Too much of a coincidence for me. Last time he wasn't supposed to have nothin' to do with our job."

"Too much of a coincidence for me too," Chaplin said. "The marshal ain't gonna like it either."

"He wouldn't like it," Saxon said, "if he knew it."

"We oughta go tell him."

"Yeah, sure," Saxon said, "and then face Spotted Dog for botherin' the old man durin' his nap?"

"You're right," Chaplin said. "Besides, the old man's so out of it these days he wouldn't even know what we were talkin' about."

"We might as well wait for Spotted Dog and tell him," Saxon said.

"You're right," Chaplin said. "Let's get back so Gar can get himself a drink."

"Or," Saxon said, "we could go back inside and get ourselves another drink."

"Gar'd be mad," Chaplin said.

"Not if we bring him back somethin'," Saxon said.

"That's a good point, Les," Chaplin said, "a damned good point."

They started back into the saloon, but then Harry Chaplin stopped and looked down the street at Clint Adams again.

"Wonder what he's doin' in town?" he said.

"If we get drunk enough," Les Saxon said, "maybe we can go ask him."

"Damned if that ain't another good point, Les."

THIRTY-EIGHT

Clint Adams came out of the livery stable and walked over to the hotel where he was staying. As soon as he entered the hotel, Spotted Dog and Frank Beckett came riding down the street, on their way to the livery stable.

Clint checked the desk register at his hotel and did not find Tolliver or his deputies. That meant they were staying at the other hotel, which was two blocks away.

He came out of his hotel and walked down the street toward the second hotel, but he didn't go in. He passed both that hotel and the Dixie Saloon and continued on to the little restaurant where he had met Deputy Sawyer.

As soon as Clint entered the restaurant, Harry Chaplin and Les Saxon came out of the Dixie, each carrying a half bottle of whiskey.

Also, Spotted Dog and Frank Beckett came walking down the street toward their hotel and spotted Chaplin and Saxon.

They had all managed to miss seeing Clint Adams completely, and vice versa.

"What the hell are you two doing out here?" Spotted Dog demanded. "You're supposed to be at the hotel watching the marshal."

"It don't take three of us to watch one old man, Dog," Les Saxon said.

Happy Chaplin opened his mouth to say something, but before he could Spotted Dog's fist crashed into Les Saxon's jaw. The man went down like he'd been poleaxed, his whiskey bottle shattering beneath him. Frank Beckett winced, wondering if the man had been cut.

Spotted Dog turned on Harry Chaplin, who said, "Wait!" He dropped his whiskey bottle and smashed it beneath his foot.

"I should kill you," Spotted Dog said.

"Wait, wait," Chaplin said, holding his hands out. "I got somethin' to tell you."

"Something that will save your life?" Spotted Dog asked.

"Jesus," Chaplin said. I hope so, he thought.

"What is it?"

"Clint Adams is in town."

"What?"

"The Gunsmith?" Frank Beckett said.

"That's right."

"Are you sure?" Spotted Dog asked. "Or are you too drunk to see straight?"

"I am too drunk to see straight, Dog, but I saw him before I got too drunk to see straight."

"Where?"

"Where what?" Chaplin asked, frowning.

"Where did you see him?"

"On the street," Chaplin said. "He was walkin' that big black of his, probably goin' to the livery."

Spotted Dog turned and looked at Beckett, who had commented on a big black they'd seen in the livery. Neither of them, however, had connected it to Clint Adams.

"That black in the barn," Beckett said now.

"Where is he now, Chaplin?" Spotted Dog asked.

"I don't know," Chaplin said, "but I'll go and find him for ya."

"No you won't," Spotted Dog said. "Take Saxon with you back to your room and you both stay there. Understand?"

"Yeah, sure, Dog."

"Then get him up!"

Beckett helped Chaplin get the unconscious man to his feet.

"He's cut," Beckett said.

"How bad?" Spotted Dog asked.

Beckett tore the man's shirt to take a look.

"Not bad. He's cut, but not stabbed."

"Wash him up when you get to your room," Spotted Dog said to Chaplin.

"Sure, Dog, sure," Chaplin said, and started half-walking, half-dragging Saxon toward the hotel.

"I'm going to the hotel too, to check on the marshal," Spotted Dog said.

"I know," Beckett said, "you want me to locate Clint Adams."

"Locate him," Spotted Dog said, "but don't talk to him. And don't let him see you. Understand?"

"I understand," Beckett said. "Some coincidence running into him again, huh?"

"It can't be a coincidence," Spotted Dog said, "not this time."

"And if it ain't?" Beckett asked. "What do we do, then?"

"Then we'll deal with him," Spotted Dog said, "the same way we deal with everything else."

"You mean kill 'im?" Beckett asked. "Kill the Gunsmith?"

"Why not?" Spotted Dog said. "Why the hell not?"

THIRTY-NINE

Spotted Dog went to Tolliver's room and found the man standing at the window, gazing out. When the marshal turned to look at him, Spotted Dog was startled. He had not seen the man look this alert in months.

"Where've you been?" Tolliver asked.

"We went out to see Craig and collect the first half of the payment."

"Who's we?"

"Beckett and me."

"Who told you to do that?"

"You did."

He was easy to lie to. He never remembered anything. Of course, it was becoming increasingly unnecessary to even lie. Most of the time he didn't even ask questions anymore.

Spotted Dog was wondering if he should mention Clint Adams to Tolliver—it would probably

151

be forgotten in a few minutes—when the marshal saved him the trouble.

"Adams is in town."

"You saw him?"

Tolliver nodded, looked back out the window, and jerked his chin.

"Out there, on the street."

"Beckett is trying to locate him."

"He went that way," Tolliver said, again using his chin to point. "My guess is he's in some restaurant, having something to eat—which is where I'd like to be."

"Marshal—"

"I want something to eat, Dog."

"I'll bring something up."

"No," Tolliver said, turning to face the Indian, "I want to go out, sit down in a restaurant, and eat."

Physically, Dan Tolliver was still an imposing presence. Ten or fifteen pounds heavier than in his prime, he did look fifty-three, but he looked like a healthy fifty-three—and in fact, he was, in every way but in his mind.

"All right, Marshal," Spotted Dog said, "let's go get something to eat."

Tolliver strapped on his gun—he still carried it, and it was still loaded. Spotted Dog often wondered if the day would come when he'd have to unload it. Tolliver picked up his hat, turned to Spotted Dog, and said, "I'm ready."

On the way downstairs Spotted Dog suggested the hotel dining room.

"Like you said," he continued, "Adams might be in a restaurant. We don't want to run into him until we're ready, do we?"

"No," Tolliver said, "that's a good point. All right, the hotel dining room it is."

Spotted Dog heaved a sigh of relief and led Tolliver to the dining room.

"Where are the others?" Tolliver asked after they had been seated and had placed their order.

"Like I said, Beckett is out looking for Adams," the Indian told him. "The others are in their rooms."

"Drunk?"

He hesitated, thought about lying, then decided there was no point.

"Two of them are."

"Chaplin and Saxon."

"Yes."

"They may have to be replaced," Tolliver said. "They do that in every town . . . don't they?"

There was a momentary flicker of fear in Tolliver's eyes, and then he seemed to bear down and fight the fog that was threatening to creep into his brain.

"Yes, they do," Spotted Dog said. Was it possible that the man he owed his life and loyalty to would fight to stay alert?

Lunch was brought to the table, and they suspended conversation while the waiter laid it all out.

"What do you think about Adams?" Tolliver asked when the waiter was gone.

"I think it's too much of a coincidence, even a year later, to run across him in a town where we have a job—again!"

"A year?" Tolliver said, looking puzzled and . . . afraid.

"Yes."

"Has it been that long?"

Even as Spotted Dog watched, a light in Dan Tolliver's eyes seemed to be dimming. There was less the light of intelligence and more the glow of fear.

"Yes, it has," he answered. "Why don't you eat before it gets cold, Marshal?"

Tolliver looked down at his food and said, "Yes . . . yes . . ."

But he made no move to do so.

"Marshal?" Spotted Dog said sadly.

"Hmm?" Tolliver jerked his head up and looked across the table at Spotted Dog, as if he were seeing him for the first time.

"Eat."

FORTY

Clint saw the man stop, peer in the front door, and then hurry away, and recognized him immediately. He didn't know the man's name, but he was sure he was one of Tolliver's men. From the way the man looked inside and then scurried away, Clint assumed that the man was actually looking for him. That meant that Tolliver knew he was in town somehow—one of his deputies might have seen him earlier—and now wanted to locate him.

Clint sat back and decided to enjoy another pot of coffee. It seemed fairly obvious now that he wouldn't have to look for Tolliver, the marshal would find him.

When Beckett returned to the hotel, he saw Spotted Dog and Tolliver leaving the dining room. From what he could see there had been no change in the marshal's condition.

As Beckett started to approach, Spotted Dog held up a hand and waved him away, then made a "wait" gesture.

Beckett sat in the lobby until Spotted Dog took Tolliver to his room and then came back down.

"Did you find him?"

"Yep. He's in a little restaurant down the street."

"Did he see you?"

"No."

"How did you spot him?"

"I stopped and looked in the door."

"And he didn't see you?"

"No . . . I don't think so."

Spotted Dog nodded and said, "He saw you, Frank."

"But I—"

"Never mind," Spotted Dog said. "Just show me where he is."

"Come on," Beckett said.

Clint wasn't surprised when Spotted Dog showed up instead of Dan Tolliver. The man he'd seen outside the restaurant was with him as well. Clint stuck a forkful of peach pie into his mouth as they approached his table.

"Pie?" he asked Spotted Dog.

"No."

"Coffee, then."

"What are you doing in town, Adams?"

"It's been a long time, Spotted Dog," he said. "How've you been? How's Tolliver?"

Spotted Dog started to reply, then turned to Beckett and said, "Wait outside."

"But, Dog—"

"Outside, Frank!"

Beckett firmed his jaw but backed away a few steps, then turned and walked out.

"Have a seat . . . *Dog*. How's the marshal? Still a little fuzzy in the head?"

"I want to know why you're here, Adams," Spotted Dog said angrily.

"I was here visiting a friend," Clint said. "Maybe you know him? Sonny Craig?"

"Just visiting, huh?" the Indian asked. "Did he try to hire you before us?"

"No," Clint said, "Craig and I were friends. In fact, I was his houseguest until I heard he was hiring you—well, your boss—to kill a man and his two children."

"Children? What are you talking about?"

"Don't you know who your targets are, Dog?" Clint asked. "One man, his nineteen-year-old daughter, and his seventeen-year-old son?"

"Rustlers," Spotted Dog said, "our target is cattle rustlers."

"That's what Craig told you," Clint said. "And in fact, there are rustlers at work here, but it isn't Frank Carmondy and his children."

"They know where the rustlers are."

Clint shook his head.

"All they did was carve up an already dead steer for meat to survive. That doesn't make them rustlers."

"There's more than one steer missing."

"I know," Clint said, "but they weren't taken by the Carmondys. They were stolen by the real rustlers."

"And do you know who these real rustlers are?"

"No," Clint said, "but if you give me some time, I'll find out, and then you can do what you were hired to do, stop some rustlers."

"We don't need you to tell us what we were hired to do, Adams," Spotted Dog said. "I don't think it's such a good idea for you to stay in Circle Creek and get involved in our business."

"You don't say."

"In fact," Spotted Dog went on, "I think it would be healthy for you to leave town."

"Not this time, Dog," Clint said. "I made a mistake in Ryland and some young men paid with their lives. I'm not going to let that happen here."

"Adams, if you don't—"

"If you go after the Carmondy family, Dog," Clint said forcefully, "you're going to have to go through me."

Spotted Dog stared at Clint for a few seconds before saying, "That's your choice, Adams."

The Indian turned and left the restaurant. Clint was committed now—and, he thought, he probably should be, for announcing that

he would stand with the Carmondys against
Tolliver and six deputies.

Outside Frank Beckett asked, "What happened?"

"I'll tell you on the way back to the hotel,"
Spotted Dog said.

He told Beckett about his conversation with
Clint Adams, and then Beckett said, "Do you
think he's right?"

"Hey," Spotted Dog said, "when did we start
deciding who's right and who's wrong? We were
hired to do a job and we're going to do it."

"Yeah, but what Adams said—"

"We're just going to have to take care of him
first," Spotted Dog said.

"How?"

"Sober up Chaplin and Saxon, then find
Rhodes and Haywood and meet me at the
Dixie Saloon in two hours."

"Sober them up in two hours?" Beckett
asked.

"And don't let them drink anything else until
I've talked to everybody."

FORTY-ONE

Two hours later, while Spotted Dog was meeting with Tolliver's men in the Dixie Saloon, Clint Adams was meeting with Sheriff Ed Tate in his office.

"You told him that?" Tate asked.

"I did."

"You put yourself right in the line of fire."

"I know."

"Was that what you intended to do?"

"To tell you the truth, Sheriff—"

"Ed."

"Ed," Clint continued, "I don't know what I intended to do. Yes, I do. I intend to see that those people aren't killed for cutting up a dead steer. I intend to see that they're not killed just so Dan Tolliver and his deputies can cut another notch and bank some more money—that is, if any of them keep their money in a bank."

"And how do you intend to stop them?" Tate asked. "Take them out one at a time?"

"No," Clint said.

"Oh, I get it," Tate said suddenly.

"You do?" Clint asked. "Then explain it to me."

"You're gonna wait until they come after you."

"All six?"

"Why not all seven?"

"No," Clint said, "not Tolliver."

"Why not?" Tate asked.

Clint had never told anyone what he knew about Dan Tolliver, but he told Sheriff Ed Tate now. Tate couldn't believe what he was hearing.

"I don't get it," Tate said. "If he was that way a year ago, he must be worse now."

"That's what I figure."

"How do they stay in business?"

"By keeping him away from people," Clint said, "by doing business without ever letting anyone they work for talk to him."

"How long can they keep that up?" Tate asked.

"Well, it's been at least a year," Clint said.

"Yeah, but how much longer?"

"Maybe," Clint said thoughtfully, "maybe until people find out about him."

Tate stared at Clint for a long moment, then nodded and said, "Oh, I get it."

And this time, so did Clint.

FORTY-TWO

In the Dixie Saloon, Spotted Dog was telling Tolliver's Deputies what had to be done. It wasn't hard to take over the saloon and empty it out because everyone knew who they were.

"Wait a minute," Carl Rhodes said. "You want us to go up against the Gunsmith?"

"That's right."

Rhodes looked around and said, "I don't know about the rest of you, but if I'm gonna go up against Clint Adams with a gun, I want a bonus."

Chaplin and Saxon exchanged a look and nodded their heads.

"Yeah," Gar Haywood said, "me too."

Beckett and Spotted Dog looked at each other. They both knew that Spotted Dog had control of Tolliver's money. They knew more about

Tolliver's infirmities of mind than any of the other men.

"Is Tolliver gonna okay that?" Saxon asked.

Could he okay it, Chaplin was wondering.

"I'll tell you what," Spotted Dog said. "There'll be a bonus for any man who puts a bullet into Clint Adams."

"When?" Rhodes asked.

"Today," Spotted Dog said, "tonight. I don't want Adams to make it to morning."

"You want us to do this together?" Rhodes asked. He had visions of back-shooting Clint Adams himself and collecting the bonus alone.

"I don't care how it gets done," Spotted Dog said, "I just want it done."

"How about a drink?" Saxon asked.

"Drink all you want," Spotted Dog said, "but remember this, any man who tries to go up against Adams drunk is going to end up dead. That's a fact."

Spotted Dog moved to a back table then, joined by Frank Beckett with a beer. He hadn't brought the Indian one because he knew he didn't drink.

"You think this is the smart thing to do?" Beckett asked Spotted Dog.

"Yes."

"But I mean . . . kill him? Just to get him out of the way?"

Spotted Dog looked at Beckett then, and the man felt a shiver from the coldness of the Indian's eyes.

"Number one, he can get in our way on this

job, and even more than that, he knows about Tolliver."

"Oh."

"If he tells anybody and the word gets around, we're finished."

"Well . . . maybe that wouldn't be a bad idea," Beckett said.

Spotted Dog just stared at him.

"Uh, tell the truth, Spotted Dog," Beckett said, "ain't you gettin' tired of coverin' for him all the time?"

Spotted Dog hesitated a few moments, then said, "You're young, Beckett. You have your whole life ahead of you. The marshal and me, we ain't so young."

"What about the others?"

Spotted Dog looked over to where Rhodes, Chaplin, Saxon, and Haywood were sitting.

"All losers," he said. "Without the marshal, they would all be dead by now."

"Well," Beckett said, "we may all be dead by morning."

"Not you and not me."

"Why not?"

"We will stay inside tonight, you and me," Spotted Dog said. "Let them trade their lives for his."

"You expect them to get killed?"

"I expect them to kill Clint Adams," Spotted Dog said. "If they are killed in the process . . ." He just shrugged.

"And what happens to the Deputies?"

"They can be replaced."

"And I can't?"

"Like I said," Spotted Dog told him, "you are young, and you've been first deputy for over a year. With the three of us, we can start again."

Frank Beckett wasn't so sure about that, but he knew better than to argue with Spotted Dog when he got like this. Maybe when this job was over, Beckett would just mount up and ride the other way.

He knew Dan Tolliver was no longer in his right mind, and now he was afraid that Spotted Dog was having the same problem.

"I can't back you up, you know," Ed Tate told Clint.

"Not officially."

"No," Tate said, shaking his head, "not at all."

"Why?"

"Why?" Tate repeated. "Hell, man, I just met you yesterday. You expect me to stick my neck out for you, and for the Carmondys? For what?"

"I expect you to do your job."

"Hey!" Tate said, slamming his hand down on his desk. "I do my job, Adams!"

"Good," Clint said, standing up, "then I have nothing to worry about, do I?"

"You have a shitload of worries, my friend," Tate said.

FORTY-THREE

Clint Adams knew he had a shitload of trouble without the sheriff telling him so. He now had six adversaries, all six of whom had experience with gun battles. Even the most inexperienced of Tolliver's men had more experience than most.

He was ready, though, but before he could be sure they'd come after him he had to do one more thing.

Coming toward him, performing his rounds, was the deputy, Kal Sawyer. Sawyer had possibly been the most use to him of anyone in town—and he could continue to do so.

"Hello, Deputy."

"Evenin', Mr. Adams."

"How are things around town tonight?"

"Oh, quiet," Sawyer said.

And he didn't waste any time being helpful, either.

"The Dixie's real quiet tonight because of Marshal Tolliver's men."

"What about the marshal's men?"

"Well, they basically took over the Dixie."

"When?"

"Just a little while ago."

"They still there?"

"I guess."

"Well," Clint said, "if they're the only ones there, I guess that means there's room at the bar, isn't there?"

"You goin' over there?" Sawyer asked, his eyes glittering with excitement.

"I guess so."

"You gonna get into it with them?"

"Get into what, Deputy?"

"I mean—well, you know." The deputy moved closer and asked, "Is there gonna be a gun-fight?"

"I sure hope not, Deputy," Clint said, "because I'm just goin' over there for a beer."

Clint started away from Sawyer, who stared after him, then decided he might as well go and tell the sheriff what was going on, just in case.

That was probably the single smartest decision he'd ever made in his life.

Clint walked over to the Dixie Saloon and found some men hanging around outside, almost kicking at the dirt in their impatience to get inside. Why they didn't just go to the other saloon, Clint didn't know—except that some people liked to do all their drinking in one place.

"Not going in?" Clint asked.

"Not until the rest of that marshal's men come out," one of the men replied.

"How many more are in there?" Clint asked.

"Two," one of the other men said, "and that mean-lookin' Injun is one of 'em."

Two, Clint repeated to himself. Well, he really did want a beer.

"Hey, mister," somebody yelled, "I wouldn't go in there if I was you."

Clint didn't bother telling the man that he wasn't him.

"He's what?" Ed Tate said, rising.

"He's walkin' over there to the Dixie Saloon where that Marshal Tolliver's men are," Sawyer said. "He says there ain't gonna be no gunfight, but, Sheriff, I think he's gonna get hisself killed!"

"Did you see what I just saw?" Chaplin asked the others.

"What?" Rhodes asked.

"What did you see?" Gar Haywood asked.

Les Saxon remained silent. They were all standing in front of their hotel, trying to decide how to go about killing Clint Adams.

"He just walked into the Dixie, bold as you please," Chaplin said.

"Who did?" Haywood asked.

"Adams," Chaplin said, pointing. "I just saw Clint Adams walk into the Dixie."

They all turned and looked toward the Dixie Saloon. There were still some men milling around outside, waiting to get in.

"Is Spotted Dog still inside?" Rhodes asked.

"Far as I know," Chaplin said.

"Didn't leave right after us," Saxon said.

"Beckett's in there with him too."

"Sure," Rhodes said, "they're stayin' where it's safe while we risk our necks for a bonus."

"I don't know about you," Saxon said, "but I want that bonus."

"Yeah," Chaplin said, "so do I."

"We all do," Rhodes said, "and maybe we're gonna get it sooner than we thought."

"Huh?" Saxon said.

"Listen . . ."

FORTY-FOUR

Clint walked into the saloon and looked around. There were three men inside. One was the bartender, who was looking at him like he was crazy. The other two were Spotted Dog and Frank Beckett.

He saw Beckett stiffen and toss a nervous glance at Spotted Dog, but the Indian remained calm. Beckett was acting like he'd seen a ghost. Clint guessed he was supposed to be dead by now.

He walked to the bar and said, "Beer."

"Mister," the bartender whispered urgently, "you don't wanna be in here—"

"Thanks for the warning, friend," Clint said, "but I really do need a beer, thanks."

The bartender studied him a moment longer, then shrugged and drew him a beer. Clint picked it up, took a quick gulp, then carried it over to the table Spotted Dog and Beckett were sharing. He noticed that there was no drink in front of Spotted Dog.

"Mind if I sit?" he asked.

"Why not?" Spotted Dog said.

Clint sat.

"Frank," Spotted Dog said, "why don't you go over and check on the men."

"Uh . . . sure, Dog, sure."

As Beckett got up and scurried out, Spotted Dog said, "The others like to drink their fill first day in town, you know? They're not doing it here, so they must be at the other saloon."

"Sure."

"What's on your mind?"

"You are," Clint said.

"We said all we had to say earlier today."

"Dog," Clint said, "what do you suppose people would think if they knew that Dan Tolliver wasn't running Tolliver's Deputies and hadn't been for a long time?"

"I don't know," Spotted Dog said, "how do you think they'd feel, Adams?"

"Well, I think some of his clients would feel a little cheated, don't you?"

"They already paid," Spotted Dog said. "Besides, they were all satisfied with our service."

"You know," Clint said, "you don't talk like any Indian I ever knew."

Spotted Dog almost smiled.

"How many have you known?"

"A few," Clint said.

"Like who?"

Clint hesitated, then said, "Quanah."

Spotted Dog's eyed widened involuntarily for a moment before he got them back under control.

"You knew Quanah Parker?"

"I did," Clint said, "and he'd be very disappointed in you, Dog. What's your white name, anyway?"

Spotted Dog firmed his jaw and said, "Never mind."

"What about future customers, Dog?" Clint asked. "How many do you think there'd be if I told what I know to a newspaperman? What kind of a legend would Dan Tolliver be then?"

"You're talking yourself into an early grave, Adams," Spotted Dog said.

"I don't think so."

"You don't, huh?"

"No, I don't," Clint said. "Do you know why?"

"Why?"

"Because I think you had already planned to kill me before I got here. I think you sent Beckett out to get the rest of the men."

"Then you're dead either way."

"Not if I go out the back," Clint said. "I don't think the back's covered, Dog. What do you think?"

The look on Spotted Dog's face told him he was right.

"You won't get far, anyway."

Clint took a healthy swallow of his beer, cocked his head, and said, "You know, I think you're right. I think I'll go out the front and face the music."

Spotted Dog suddenly looked satisfied.

"Good move."

"Get up," Clint said, standing up.

"Why?"

"Why? Because you're coming with me, that's why. You don't think I'm going to step out onto that street alone, do you?"

Spotted Dog didn't move.

"Come on, get up, Dog."

The Indian slid his chair back, but he still did not get up. Clint knew he was thinking about going for the knife on his hip. He knew the look.

"Go ahead, Dog," he invited, "go ahead and try me all by yourself."

They matched stares for a few moments, and then Clint saw the shadow of doubt pass over Spotted Dog's face.

"Drop the pigsticker on the floor. Now Dog."

Spotted Dog hesitated, then dropped his knife to the floor.

"Now stand up and let's go outside."

The Indian stood up, and Clint moved around behind him and said, "You first."

"Scared?" Spotted Dog asked with a sneer.

"Cautious," Clint said. "Learn the difference, Dog—if you live long enough."

FORTY-FIVE

Outside Beckett had found the other men, all of whom were looking for a good vantage point.

"Move 'em around, Carl," Beckett said.

"Sure, First Dep," Rhodes said. He still thought the job should be his, and after this maybe it would be.

He turned and said to Haywood, "Get rid of all these other men and then take cover."

Haywood cleared the area of the waiting drinkers, then took cover.

"Start shooting as soon as you see him," Rhodes told Haywood, Saxon, and Chaplin.

"Are we goin' over?" Sawyer asked.

"Why?" Tate asked.

"To help him."

"Why should we?" Tate demanded, but he knew the answer. It was his job.

"Sheriff—"

"Shit, yeah," Tate said, strapping on his gun belt, "let's go."

As they neared the door, Clint stopped.

"What's wrong?"

"I changed my mind," Clint said. "I'm going out first."

"You?"

"That's right," Clint said. "Stand beside me. I'm going to step out, and then you right after me. Understand?"

Spotted Dog didn't understand, but he liked the idea. He wouldn't even have to try anything. Clint Adams was doing the job for him.

"Whatever you say."

They approached the batwing doors abreast, and Clint knew that his timing was going to have to be perfect. He took a deep breath, pushed the doors aside with his right arm, and stepped out with his left hand tightly clasped around Spotted Dog's elbow.

He heard a click and reacted. He yanked on Spotted Dog, pulling him through the batwing doors and pushing him in front of him.

"No!" the Indian shouted, but it was too late. It was approaching dusk, and flashes could be seen in the dying light as Tolliver's Deputies started shooting.

• • •

Chunks of lead thudded into Spotted Dog's body, causing him to dance about long after his heart had stopped. It wasn't until the shooting had ceased that he fell.

Clint sighted in on one of the muzzle flashes and fired. Somebody shouted in pain, and then the firing started again as he dove for cover.

"You fired too soon!" Beckett shouted. "You killed Spotted Dog!"

"Fire! Fire! Get Adams!" Rhodes shouted.

They all started firing again, except for Les Saxon. Clint's bullet had pierced his heart and killed him on the spot.

Tate and Sawyer came on the scene as Beckett, Rhodes, and the others had Clint pinned down.

"Jesus!" Sawyer said.

"Go around, Kal," Tate said. "Take the alley and go around. When I start firing, you start firing. Got it?"

"I understand, Sheriff."

"And for God's sake be careful!" Tate shouted after him.

Clint reloaded, realizing he was pinned down good. He couldn't even make it back into the saloon. All he had between the rest of the deputies and himself was a horse trough that was punched full of holes and emptying of water.

When the water was gone, there wouldn't be much cover left.

He was going to have to make some kind of move.

Ed Tate waited what he thought was enough time for Sawyer to work his way around to the other side. If he waited any longer, it would be dark and difficult to see. He had to act now.

He took out his gun, sighted down on one of Tolliver's Deputies, and fired. With all the shooting going on, he couldn't tell if Sawyer was firing or not, but it was too late to worry.

Haywood felt a bullet punch into his right side. How'd that happen? Adams was in front of them. He turned that way, saw the sheriff, but not in time to react. Tate fired a second time, and the bullet drove into Haywood's chest.

On the other side Chaplin suddenly realized that Haywood was down from gunfire to the right. He stood, saw the sheriff, and aimed, but before he could fire, a bullet struck him from the left, spinning him around and dumping him on the ground.

"Christ!" Beckett shouted, suddenly realizing that not only were there others firing at them now, but they were suddenly outnumbered. Only he and Rhodes were left.

"Get out of here, Carl! Let's get out of here!"

"Run, you lily-livered—" Rhodes started shouting at Beckett, the man who had held his job for a year. "Go ahead and run—"

Clint fired, his bullet hitting Frank Beckett's spine.

Carl Rhodes, seeing he was alone, screamed and charged toward Clint. Three guns fired, and all hit their mark. Rhodes fell facedown in the center of the street.

Clint stepped out from his cover, and he and the two lawmen converged around the fallen Rhodes.

"Glad you could make it, Sheriff."

Tate looked at Clint and said, "Ed, remember?"

Sheriff Tate opened the hotel room door with a key obtained from the desk clerk. Sawyer was outside, presiding over the cleanup. Tate and Clint entered the room where Marshal Dan Tolliver was lying on the bed on his back, asleep. His gun belt was hanging on the bedpost.

"Think he'll be any trouble?" Tate asked.

"Tolliver!" Clint called out. The man didn't move, so he jarred the bed with his foot. "Tolliver!"

The man's eyes fluttered, then opened and stayed open. He turned his head and looked directly at Clint Adams. Clint had never before seen eyes with such a vacant look in them.

"Who are you?" Tolliver asked.

Clint looked at Tate and said, "No trouble at all."

Watch for

ORPHAN TRAIN

154th in the exciting GUNSMITH series
from Jove

Coming in October!